UNBELIEVABLY PUZZLED

THE PUZZLED MYSTERY ADVENTURE SERIES: BOOK 9

P.J. Nichols

Paperback ISBN 978-4-910091-36-5
Hardcover ISBN 978-4-910091-37-2

pjnichols.com

Cover design by Thomas Paehler

For The Puzzled Series readers,
I hope you enjoy reading this story as much
as I enjoyed writing it!

CHAPTER 1

"Good morning, Mr. Sullivan," Peter said politely as he walked into his chemistry classroom at 8:10 on a chilly winter morning. "We're still doing our first lab today, right?"

"Yes, indeed," his teacher replied with a grin.

Peter's schedule for his second term of Grade 11, which had only begun last week, was filled with classes and teachers he was pretty excited about. Rumor had it that Mr. Sullivan was one of the best chemistry teachers in the whole district, and he was well-known for tailoring assignments to challenge even the cleverest of students.

In Peter's mind, fully understanding chemistry—the science he considered to be the *basis of all life*—was crucial to give him an advantage after finishing high school (regardless of which of the sciences he chose to specialize in down the road.)

Class didn't start until half past eight, so Peter had a good twenty minutes to kill before the bell.

With only two other students currently in the room, neither of whom Peter knew well, there was little to do other than let his mind wander...

* * *

The dynamics of Peter—Neil—Claire—Nicola had transformed significantly since their mission to Axon a couple of months back.

Peter and Neil were once again good buddies, and they hung out a lot both at and outside of school. Neither had officially apologized for shunning the other for so long, but both knew they were much better off now as friends again.

Peter and Claire's relationship had dissolved immediately after returning from Axon. And their undiscussed decision to break up had precipitated from events during that amulet-seeking adventure. (She had not only been rude to Nicola numerous times, but had even forcefully knocked her to the ground once.) When Peter had questioned Claire about that unprovoked attack, she simply twisted her head to the side and said, "Whatever." And since that comment, the two had yet to speak again.

At more or less the same time as the Claire break-up, Peter and Nicola had begun a *quasi-relationship* type of thing, where they were somewhere in the grey zone between being friends and being a couple. They hung out a fair bit at school, chatted on the phone a few times a week, and got together occasionally on weekends. They sometimes even held hands while walking around (outside of school), but there had been no kissing at all.

And Claire (for reasons unknown) seemed to once again be after Neil. (Neil told Peter that Claire phoned him a lot these days and was keen on getting back together.) Since she kept persisting, Neil replied by saying he was up for the occasional date, but that he was going to be dating other girls as well. (Neil was NOT interested in having a steady girlfriend.) Claire had been relatively satisfied with that proposal, so she and Neil would get together every now and then.

* * *

"Hey, Pete," Nicola said out of nowhere, ending Peter's little daydream session.

"Hey," he replied happily. "What are you doing here? You're not thinking of dropping drama class and taking chem instead, are you?"

"Absolutely not," she laughed. "I just came by to tell you I'm meeting up with Stacy and Caroline at lunch. We're working on our first minidrama performance, which we have to do in front of our class this Friday."

"Gotcha," Peter smiled.

"Okay, later," she smiled back while heading out. "I'll call you tonight."

* * *

With another ten minutes left before the bell, Peter got out his notebook. (Not the one for chemistry class; The one he used to keep detailed memos related to weather god stuff.)

After checking over both shoulders to make sure no one was looking his way, he opened it up to his *list:* This list included things he considered vital to keep close tabs on, and notes about the current status of each one.

· *Size of our combined army (from Sevlar and Chronostil): 142*

· *News about Mr. Winchester: nothing*

· *Update from Zoltan: he spoke to the lead weather gods, and the government is pondering whether or not to recruit Sevlarians to help us*

· *News about Xavier: nothing*

· *Incidents/accidents on Earth: none*

With Mr. Winchester still on Axon (and Zoltan trapped on Sevlar), Demetrius had kind of taken over as the leader of the crew at Mr. Winchester's home.

Peter went over regularly so they could keep him updated on any new developments. Plus, they could also brainstorm when/if/how to engage Xavier. Since Klaron was also trapped on Sevlar, the crew from Chronostil was a bit disorganized and disgruntled. There had not been a second-in-command to Klaron, so instead of appointing a new leader, they elected to have four of Klaron's closest subordinates play that role together. (But these four had quite opposing views, so they often just bickered amongst themselves.)

* * *

"When are we going to do this?" Peter mumbled to himself at his desk. The *"this"* he was talking about was initiating an attack on Xavier. They had been planning it judiciously for weeks, but a few more pieces of the puzzle had to fall into place first...

"Looks like everyone has arrived," Mr. Sullivan announced to the whole class, closing the door just before the bell was set to ring. "Make sure you're sitting with your lab partner, the pairs I assigned you before."

* * *

The only one of the twenty-three students in the class without an assigned partner was Peter, and that was a mutual decision reached between Peter and Mr. Sullivan. (His teacher felt that pairing Peter up with another student—knowing that Peter was both a perfectionist and extremely good with science—would lead to his partner just sitting back and twiddling his or her thumbs while Peter did everything. Then that pupil would end up getting a perfect score for each and every lab, without understanding even a fraction of what experiment they had done.)

When his teacher asked Peter if he would mind working alone on labs, Peter happily obliged. (This also meant that he wouldn't have to worry about his partner botching things up.)

* * *

"Now please reread the instructions for today's experiment," Mr. Sullivan said to the class. "And start setting up everything necessary at your stations. I'll be back in about five minutes."

* * *

When Mr. Sullivan returned to the class seven minutes later, a young man (presumably a student who had just transferred to Clearview High) was beside him.

"Everyone," his teacher announced. "This is Frederick. His family has just moved here from Lemmington, and he had been attending St. Alastair Academy."

A few oohs and aahs could be heard around the class, as Lemmington was a massive, bustling city compared to the tiny town of Clearville. Not only that, but St. Alistair Academy was an expensive private school right in the center of Lemmington. Most Clearville families didn't have even half of the money required for the tuition fees there.

There were also a few tiny giggles here and there, coming from the insensitive students who thought Frederick's appearance and attire were a little weird. (He wasn't wearing his previous school's uniform, but he did show up today in slacks, dress shoes, a collared shirt, and a nice blazer.)

"Knock it off," Peter whispered to the rude kid beside him. "Give him a chance, man. He just moved here."

"Please call me Freddy," the young man said to his new classmates, looking a little uncomfortable. "I look forward to getting to know you all."

"Peter," Mr. Sullivan said next. "Since you have no lab partner, would you mind pairing up with Frederick? Sorry, I mean *Freddy.*"

"Not at all," Peter replied politely. He was being genuine when saying that, as he had already noticed a similarity between himself and this new kid: likely a clever boy who was also teased a lot while growing up.

"Wonderful," the teacher smiled. "Freddy, please join Peter over there. He'll help get you up to speed."

"Thank you, sir," Frederick replied (without realizing that students weren't required to call their teachers *'Sir'* or *'Ma'am'* like at his previous educational institution.

* * *

Since today's entire class was for the lab, Peter and Frederick had plenty of time to chat while doing the experiment. (And to Peter's surprise, Frederick was amazingly capable and knowledgeable as far as science went. His new classmate certainly excelled academically.)

Frederick's story was partly intriguing and partly sad. The sad part was the reason his family had suddenly moved to Clearville. His father, only 51 (and now the *former* CEO of a massive financial firm) had had a massive heart attack last fall while at the office. Quick response by medical professionals, followed by successful quadruple bypass surgery had meant his dad was alive and well, but the specialist blamed the heart attack on work-related stress. The surgeon's comment terrified Frederick's father, so he took early retirement (which included enough financial compensation that he would never have to work again.)

(But why Clearville?)

Well, Frederick explained the reasons for that. One: it was a small town, with a relaxing atmosphere, and there were no big companies here that might give his dad the urge to rejoin the workforce. And two: Frederick's older sister was attending Stoneburg Technological, only a 20-minute drive away. She had been living in the dormitory, but was now back with her family and made the commute to school every morning by car.

* * *

"Where's your locker?" Peter asked Frederick

as they cleaned up the supplies after the successful chem experiment. "Wanna meet up at lunch?"

"Sure," Frederick replied happily. "It's near room 116."

"Cool, I know where that is," Peter told him. "Just hang there until I show up."

"Superb," Frederick replied, happy to have made an acquaintance on his first day.

CHAPTER 2

Just as Peter had expected, his two closest friends had been awesomely welcoming to the new kid from the big city. Peter had introduced Frederick to Nicola and Neil the day after he met him in chem class, and now (three weeks later), Frederick was hanging out with them at school like they'd known each other for ages.

Frederick had even joined Neil and Peter for an evening of burgers and pool. And tonight, (his third Friday since moving to Clearville), the three boys and Nicola were going out for pizza and a movie.

"Thanks for inviting me again tonight," Frederick said as they sat down at one of the six tables at everyone's favorite little pizza place in Clearville. "It's very kind of you to bring me along everywhere."

"Dude," Neil laughed. "You gotta quit thanking us for being your friend."

"No kidding," Nicola said next, smiling. "We

like hanging out with you."

"And get this," Peter mentioned. "Freddy here has one-upped me as far as chem grades go. I've got a 100% average so far, but he's got 102%."

"102?" Neil replied, laughing. "Oh man, don't tell me we've got another *Pete* on our hands here."

"Hold up," Nicola giggled. "How can anyone have an average over 100?"

"On each big test," Peter answered, "Mr. Sullivan adds a very tricky bonus question to the end."

"And YOU couldn't answer it?" Neil smiled. "Freddy my man, give me a high-five! You have officially dethroned Pete as Clearville's #1 genius!"

Frederick looked a little embarrassed, but he was so happy about how well he was fitting in so far. "Actually," he said, "that title should go to my sister. She is WAY smarter than I could ever dream of becoming."

"How old is your sister?" Neil asked.

"Seventeen," he answered.

"Seventeen?" Neil asked back. "Then why isn't she in Grade 12?"

"She was given special permission to enter Stoneburg Tech after finishing Grade 11 at St. Alistair," Frederick explained. "Like I said, she is mega-intelligent."

"Wow," Nicola commented. "Two natural brainiacs in the same family. You guys should form your own research firm or something when you get older."

"I bet he's gonna tell us they've already laid out the groundwork for that," Neil joked.

Frederick started laughing.

"No way, dude!" Neil said loudly, shaking his head. "You and your sis are already up to something big, aren't you?"

"The phase *something big* would be an exaggeration," Frederick admitted. "But thanks to my dad's business connections, my sister and I published a book together last year."

"A book?" Nicola reacted. "About what?"

"Promise me you won't laugh when I tell you," Frederick said to everyone.

The three looked back and forth at each other.

"Don't worry, man," Neil told Frederick. "No judging here."

"Okay," Frederick went on. "My sister and I have always loved doing tricky questions, like the bonus ones on Mr. Sullivan's tests. They make you rack your brains and apply puzzle-solving skills. So we came up with a whole bunch of original, like... *challenging puzzles*. Puzzles that people can only solve by unraveling clues or interpreting things in a certain way, et cetera."

"Puzzles!?" all three reacted at the same time.

"Yup," Frederick told them.

"Did you get rich from it yet?" Neil asked.

"In my dreams," Frederick replied. "I think my dad only supported the idea because the *aggressive businessman* ingrained in his DNA wanted us to see firsthand how the publishing process works."

"How much is one copy?" Peter asked.

"$9.99" Frederick replied.

Peter pulled out his wallet and removed a 10-dollar bill. "Bring me mine on Monday morning," he told Frederick. "I can't wait to see it."

"You guys like puzzles, too?" he asked.

"Like??" Nicola roared. "We LOVE puzzles! We have done more puzzles than you could possibly imagine!"

* * *

After dropping Frederick off at home—(Neil had borrowed his mom's car for the evening)—the three friends were kind of speechless at first.

"Well," Neil said, getting ready to share his opinion. "Tell me I'm not the only one here who thinks we need him on our team."

"I'm convinced too," Nicola said next. "I mean, he's already our friend, smarter than Pete, and he's published a book full of puzzles!"

"Do you think he'd help us?" Neil then asked. "I mean, it's pretty dangerous. Plus, he might just think we are all crazy if we tell him about the weather gods."

"Oh, he'll definitely help," Nicola smiled. "I saw the sparkle in his eye the second I mentioned how much we love puzzles."

"It would be awesome to have his help," Peter

agreed. "But we've only known him for a few weeks. I think telling him now would scare him off. It's pretty overwhelming stuff."

"Well, then let's wait a little longer before saying anything," Nicola suggested. "But getting him on board should be a high priority for us."

"I agree," Neil nodded.

CHAPTER 3

Today (Saturday morning) meant that—just like all other Saturday mornings—Peter was heading to Mr. Winchester's home for the weekly meeting.

Three of the people who had always been essential members of these meetings were, of course, no longer in attendance. (Mr. Winchester was still recovering on Axon. Plus, Zoltan and Klaron had been exiled to Sevlar.) Demetrius had, without being persuaded at all, taken over as the head honcho, mainly because he wouldn't (couldn't?) rest until his son Zoltan returned safe and sound.

Torin was regularly communicating with those he could still contact on Sevlar, making sure he was always up to date on Xavier's latest moves.

Aurora, Maximilian, and Cynthia had been training day after day with the giant group from Chronostil, experimenting with different ways of combining powers to create bigger storms than one weather god could do on his or her own. (And thankfully, their skills were progressing leaps and bounds.)

One of Peter's big fears, *('How's everyone from Chronostil gonna act without Klaron around?')*, was luckily working out fine. Since no one in the Chronostil group was confident enough to state their views strongly like Klaron always did, they rarely opposed ideas suggested by Demetrius.

* * *

The instant Peter walked into Mr. Winchester's home today, he knew something was up. There was a type of tension (and quietness) in the living room that he had never seen before.

"Peter," Sapphire said, briefly breaking the silence. "I'll bring you a coffee soon; I just started brewing a fresh pot. There's a lot you need to catch up on in there."

* * *

The weekly meetings typically never got underway until after Peter arrived, but something had obviously been discussed before he walked through the door this morning.

"Peter," Torin said, standing up. "We've had some... well, unnerving developments."

"But remember, Torin," Cynthia added, wanting to make sure Peter didn't get overly anxious before hearing what was going to be explained. "Your informants back on Sevlar were making some inferences, so all this is not a rock-solid fact."

"True," Torin nodded. "Peter, as I just finished telling everyone here, we received some worrisome news from Grygor, my contact on Sevlar."

"An upcoming attack?" Peter asked, pulse well over 120 bpm already. "How soon will they get here? How many ships? When did they depart?"

"Thankfully," Demetrius said from the sofa. "No one is coming. Not yet, at least."

"In my most recent communique with Grygor," Torin went on. "It was explained to me that Xavier suddenly halted his recruiting efforts."

"He just... like, stopped?" Peter asked. "Why?"

"Well, there's more," Torin continued. "Shortly after that, numerous ships from Xavier's fleet were spotted converging in one hanger on Sevlar. And these vessels are currently undergoing checks and repairs. Oh, and by numerous, we're talking upward of thirty ships."

"Then they'll be heading here pretty soon," Peter gulped. "Xavier must have determined his army is big enough that he can't lose."

"Yes, that is highly likely," Demetrius said sadly.

"Any idea of when they might depart?" Peter then asked.

"Now this is all just guesswork," Torin answered. "But we know they have at least 100 ships in total. If they have yet to even begin servicing the other 70—which would require a reasonable amount of time to do—I would say we're safe for a week at least, possibly two."

"But they could, on the contrary, be planning to attack in waves," Cynthia chimed in. "Meaning the first onslaught could come anytime."

"Wish there was some good news…" Peter said. "You know, something positive from Zoltan or Mr. Winchester."

"We still hear from Zoltan almost every day," Demetrius told Peter. "And his effort to convince the government to send weather gods to help us is progressing."

"Yes, he is making some headway," Torin added. "But he said he feels like he is always walking on eggshells."

"Because of that poison-filled thing on his wrist, right?" Peter inquired.

"Well, that too," Torin answered. "But his biggest challenge is finding opportunities to speak to the *'trustworthy'* lead weather gods when Argon, who we know is on Xavier's payroll, isn't around."

"Indeed," Demetrius added. "And then everyone Zoltan speaks to has to keep up the facade of not knowing Argon's true allegiance."

"Isn't Argon getting suspicious of anything?" Peter asked.

"From what Zoltan tells us," Demetrius answered, "he's oblivious to what's going on."

"Which is essential," Peter nodded. "Xavier would go nuclear if he knew what we are up to."

"And regarding Leonardo," Demetrius (Mr. Winchester's lifelong friend) said sadly. "We have heard nothing. But that doesn't necessarily mean something is wrong. We just have no way of getting in touch."

"Mr. Winchester knows what's at stake," Peter said calmly, stating his view. "He'll do what's required of him as soon as he can. When we hear from him next, it will be to tell us the exact news we are waiting for."

"You sure seem confident," Maximilian remarked. "Remember, Leonardo isn't as young as he used to be."

"Age may have slowed his body down," Peter smiled. "But his mind is still in tip-top shape."

CHAPTER 4

When Peter got back to his empty house just before noon, there was a note sitting on the kitchen table.

Pete,

Please call Freddy,

He mentioned something about going to Stoneburg Technological on Monday?

Love, Mom

Peter's mind quickly jumped out of *worrying about Xavier mode* when he saw the note. (A chance to visit Stoneburg Tech! Really!?)

Just like he always did, Peter tried to decipher exactly what the message could be referring to. (Monday was a professional development day, meaning no classes for high school kids. But how would that translate into a trip to one of the country's top science institutions?)

Peter was great at memorizing so many things, but people's phone numbers were not one of those… He went upstairs (to his room) to check Frederick's number, which he had recently added to the list on his corkboard.

* * *

"Pete!" Frederick said cheerfully into the receiver. "Thanks for calling back."

"My mom mentioned something about making a trip to Stoneburg Tech on Monday?" Peter asked excitedly.

"Ah, yes," Frederick replied. "I thought that would pique your interest, seeing how highly you regard that school. So, get this, I talked to my sister, and she said we can join her on Monday."

"Join her? Are you serious?" Peter asked, really giddy now. "You mean, like, attend class with her?"

"Precisely," Frederick told his friend. "She has already asked her professors, and they said we are welcome to attend her morning lectures. She's got one at 9:30 and one at 10:30. Then we'll eat lunch with her. And when she has her 2-hour lab in the afternoon, we just tour around the campus on our own."

"This is so awesome!" Peter cheered. "You sure she doesn't mind?"

"Not at all," Frederick replied. "She is excited to meet you, too. Especially after I told her you wanted a copy of the book. Anyway, she usually leaves here around half past eight, so we'll pick you up a little after that."

"No, I'll come to your place," Peter insisted. "I don't want your sis to have to go out of her way in the morning before school: My house is the opposite way from Stoneburg."

"Sure, if you don't mind," Frederick answered. "Okay, we'll see you on Monday morning then. Enjoy the rest of your weekend."

"Thanks, man," Peter replied. "You, too!"

CHAPTER 5

Peter was so excited about his upcoming trip to Frederick's sister's college that he could barely concentrate on anything all day Sunday. (It took him close to two hours to complete his homework, which he easily could have finished in less than half that time if his mind wasn't wandering so much.)

Plus, no matter how many times he tried, he couldn't make any headway on brainstorming ideas for what to do if Xavier attacked before Mr. Winchester was ready…

* * *

After an unbelievably restless night, Peter decided to get dressed and eat breakfast early the next morning. (Well, not just *early…* he was completely ready to head out an hour before he needed to be!)

"Hey, Pete," his mom said. "You look like you have some free time on your hands this morning."

Peter knew a chore was about to be thrown his

way… But he also wanted to stay on his mom's good side, since he knew his parents were going on a private getaway next weekend (and he didn't want to be assigned some massive tasks while they were gone.)

"Yeah, I don't have to be at Freddy's until 8:30," he told her.

"Would you mind starting the laundry, then?" his mom asked. "But please don't wash the dark clothes together with the light ones, like your dad always does. I don't need any more of my white t-shirts turning pink or light blue."

"Yes, boss," Peter smiled, heading to the laundry room.

"And I suggest you pinch your nose or hold your breath while throwing Brad's sports gear in," his mom added. "It stinks something awful."

(Peter giggled to himself, briefly wondering how Xavier's team would react if they were hit with a bag of Bradley's sweaty socks!)

* * *

Ding-dong

After pushing the front doorbell of Frederick's home just before 8:30, Peter took a few steps back, expecting Frederick and his sister to come outside.

"Good morning, Peter," Frederick's dad said politely while opening the front door and welcoming him inside. "Well, it would appear Freddy forgot to phone you last night."

"Freddy!" his mom yelled upstairs. "You didn't call Peter, did you?"

Peter, a little uncomfortable, softly asked, "I'm sorry, is everything alright?"

"Freddy came down with a fever yesterday afternoon," his mom explained. "He was supposed to call and tell you he would unfortunately have to cancel today's trip."

"Sorry!" Frederick yelled from his bedroom. "I guess I fell asleep!"

"We're sorry, Peter," his mom apologized. "He's so forgetful and—"

"No big deal," Peter told the apologetic parents. "I'm just sorry to hear Freddy's not feeling well."

"Mom!" Frederick's sister yelled from her room upstairs. "Don't send Pete home, he can still come with me today!"

"Peter?" his dad asked.

"Um…" Peter thought.

"Come on, Pete!" Frederick's sister yelled again. "It'll be fun! You're gonna love my profs!"

"Thanks!" Frederick called to his sister from his bedroom. "I owe you one!"

"Be down in a minute, Pete!" his sister then said.

"Okay, no rush," Peter replied.

* * *

Frederick's dad went back to finish cooking the scrambled eggs he had previously put in the frying pan, and his mom chatted pleasantly with Peter while waiting for her daughter to come downstairs.

* * *

"All set!" his sister said a few minutes later after emerging from her room. "Nice to meet you, Pete. I'm Valerie. Call me Val, though."

"Okay," Peter replied, lifting his head up to look at Frederick's sister.

The instant he saw Valerie, two completely opposing things happened at the exact same time: His body froze, but his heart started racing.

Peter could think of no better phrase to describe Valerie with than *'drop-dead gorgeous.'* He had seen beautiful girls in the movies and on TV, but had never actually stood so close to someone this attractive.

"Here's your copy of the book," she said as she got to the bottom step, holding it out for Peter. "And here's your ten bucks back. My dad said there is no way he's taking money from one of Freddy's friends. Consider it on the house."

* * *

Valerie's wonderfully friendly personality (and keenness to hear more about Peter's love of puzzles and science) quickly helped him feel relaxed while they drove to her college.

She also thanked Peter over and over again for being so nice to her brother. Apparently, Frederick was over the moon about already having a few close friends.

* * *

"Here we go," Valerie said while leading him to her first lecture of the day. "Advanced Chem 122. You're going to love Dr. Rosenthal."

"Can't wait," Peter said, following her into the medium-sized lecture hall.

Valerie said a few *"Hi's"* and *"Hey's"* to the people she knew well in her class, and introduced Peter to each person she spoke to.

"Shouldn't I just sit in the back row?" Peter asked, noticing they were getting closer and closer to the front.

"Not a chance!" she laughed, lightly punching his left shoulder. "You're sitting right next to me, in the front, of course!"

Her professor had arrived early to set things up for his lecture.

"Good morning, Dr. Rosenthal," she said as she and Peter sat down. "This is my brother's friend, Peter, who I told you about earlier. Thank you again for allowing him to join us today."

"This young man needs no introduction," the elderly professor grinned upon recognizing Peter's face. "We most certainly know of him."

He came over and shook Peter's hand.

"Peter here," the professor went on, "has consistently scored in the top percentile on the national achievement test year after year. And he has won more science competitions than I can count. I was even a judge at one he participated in a few years back, in which his rising sea level display and presentation blew the rest of the displays out of the water, no pun intended."

"Wow!" Valerie grinned. "Pete, you're already more famous here than I am."

Peter's face turned red.

"And I trust I'll see your hand raised at least a few times in today's lecture, Peter?" Dr. Rosenthal mentioned while heading back to the lectern. "If you are anything like Valerie here, I can expect quite a barrage of questions."

* * *

Dr. Rosenthal's lecture, which focused on mass spectrometry, was so intriguing that Peter even took out a notebook to jot a few things down.

* * *

At the end of the lecture, Dr. Rosenthal came up and thanked them for all the tough questions.

"Peter," the professor said just before they stood up to leave. "I certainly hope to see you in the front row of my class two years from now. If you ever have any questions about our science program, stop by my office anytime."

* * *

Valerie's 10:30 lecture—Advanced Physics 132—was also very interesting, although some of the concepts (and complex mathematics required) left Peter a little bewildered. (This was, quite possibly, the first time he had ever left a classroom confused about what he had been taught.)

* * *

"Told you Dr. Jacobs races through material," Valerie said to Peter as they left the lecture hall. "Mind you, he always recommends going through the readings BEFORE each lecture, which I did carefully last night. So, in all fairness, it kind of makes sense he lost you halfway in. Hey, on another topic, you must be hungry?"

"Starving," Peter replied. (He had been so excited in the morning that his stomach had only allowed him to consume half of his breakfast.)

"Then we are heading to Cafe Italiana," Valerie told him. "Lunch is on me!"

* * *

The place they ate at was an off-campus pizza/pasta/coffee house, big enough that they could stay for a good hour and a half without taking up space for other customers.

Valerie loved hearing how Peter had been a puzzler his whole life; a trait he shared with both her and Frederick. They laughed away all lunch, comparing stories of some of the crazy puzzles they had made up as kids. (Peter, of course, had to avoid saying anything related to *weather god stuff...*)

* * *

"Yikes, time flies," Valerie said when she noticed it was a little past one o'clock. "I gotta head back. My lab is from 1:30 to 3:30. Feel free to chill wherever you want." Then she reached into her backpack and pulled out a map of the campus.

"I put stars on some of the spots I thought you might want to check out."

"Cook, thanks," Peter replied. "Where should I meet up with you after your lab?"

"In the lobby of the main library," she answered. "It's super close to where my lab building is, and there are tons of benches to sit on in there."

"Gotcha," Peter answered.

"Oh, and if you happen to get bored," she smiled. "Then try the puzzle on page 26 of that book Freddy and I wrote."

"Are the solutions in the back?" Peter asked.

"Nope," she laughed. "Well, the solutions technically come in a little answer key in the back, but I removed it from the copy I gave you." Then she smiled while getting ready to jog to class. "So you'll have to run your answers by me or Freddy. Alright, later!"

CHAPTER 6

Frederick's fever had come down on Monday evening, but his appetite had yet to return, so his parents figured it was safest to keep him home from school on Tuesday as well. (Frederick had protested profusely, as he hated missing any school.)

* * *

When he returned to Clearville High on Wednesday morning and was heading to his locker, he saw Peter standing there waiting for him.

"Freddy! You're alive!" Peter exclaimed, high-fiving his friend.

"Well, I technically lost 1.2 kilograms over the past few days due to lack of proper eating," Frederick explained. "But I did manage to finish about 80% of my breakfast this morning."

"What a statistical response," Peter laughed. "Anyway, it's good to have you back, man."

"Thanks," Frederick smiled. "And by the way, it seems you made quite an impression on Monday."

Peter, for a brief second, imagined (wished!) that Frederick was referring to Valerie being impressed by his masculinity. But no, he was talking about Valerie's professors knowing who Peter was before being introduced.

"But I think her chemistry prof," Peter said, "Dr. Rosenthal, only remembered me because he judged a science competition a few years back."

"Stop being humble," Frederick remarked. "Val specifically said her profs knew of ALL your achievements."

"Oh, and before I forget," Peter said, handing Frederick a small collection of photocopied sheets. "Here's all the stuff you missed yesterday. I made copies of everything."

"Thanks!" he replied, looking truly happy. "But you're only in two of my classes. How did you get the rest?"

"I went to see all your other teachers after school yesterday," Peter told him. "I asked them to show me what you missed."

"Wow," Frederick smiled. "That was nice of you."

"Hey, man," Peter replied. "What are friends for?"

(But while saying that, part of Peter's mind was thinking about how Frederick's sister was the hottest girl on the planet... and she was smart... and she loved puzzles...)

CHAPTER 7

When Peter started heading home from school on Friday afternoon, he felt pretty burnt out (even though it had only been a 4-day week.) The reason for this uncommon exhaustion was simple: he had spent the majority of his time over the past few days fantasizing about Valerie. (One of his teachers had even asked Peter if he was feeling alright, since her *typically attentive student* had looked so lost in his thoughts…)

* * *

About halfway home, Peter saw Neil walking toward him from far away, which seemed a little weird. Why would Neil be heading TO school now? (The bell to dismiss them had only rung ten minutes ago. Plus, Peter knew that school was the last place Neil wanted to be…)

"Dude!" Peter yelled, waving to his buddy. "What did you forget at school?"

Neil only briefly looked at Peter, but didn't wave or reply.

"Yo! Neil!" Peter called again, figuring his friend was pretending to ignore him so he could suddenly tackle him by surprise at the last second. "Not cleaning your ears these days?"

...

Peter then stopped as Neil was just about to pass by him. "Neil, this is what you get for having so many girlfriends at once," he joked. "Never a peaceful moment to relax."

"Look, pal," the voice (which was not Neil's!) replied. "You're too young to be drunk, so you must just be crazy. I have no idea who *Neil* is, but *I ain't him.*"

"Sorry, sir," Peter mumbled in embarrassment. "You just look so much like—"

As the man kept going, Peter realized that this person was taller, older, and had longer hair than his best friend. (But this guy's clothing and walk had been so close to Neil's that he seemed like a true doppelganger.)

CHAPTER 8

When Peter walked through the front door of his home, he noticed immediately that his house was now "decorated" with tons of little square 3-inch papers. Each of these small, yellow notes had a simple (and in most cases, ridiculously obvious) instruction written on it.

"Lock the deadbolt before bed," Peter mumbled, reading the one on the inside of the front door. "How stupid does she think we are?"

"Would your really like me to answer that?" his mom said sarcastically from the living room. She had one small suitcase and her backpack lined up beside the sofa. (And her hat, sunglasses, and jacket were all neatly laid out as well.)

"By that confused expression on your face," she remarked. "You have clearly forgotten that your father and I are heading to the coast for our anniversary getaway."

"Is that THIS weekend?" Peter—who had indeed not remembered—asked.

"It's written on the calendar," his mom pointed out. "We are leaving at about five. And c'mon, I packed my bags a few days ago. Didn't you notice them here by the sofa?"

"Oh..." Peter replied. "Where's Dad? Still at work?"

"No, he's packing for our trip the only way he knows how," his mom laughed. "He's in the bedroom, madly throwing a mess of stuff into his bag, at the last minute... I wonder how many things he'll forget this time?"

"When do you get back?" Peter asked next.

"Also indicated on the calendar," she informed her son. "Monday afternoon."

"You guys don't work on Monday?" Peter inquired.

"No, we both took the day off," she answered. "Sheesh, I can see you inherited your father's memory. Or lack thereof..."

"Then I should consider myself lucky to have a mom that is so considerate that she writes reminder notes and posts them all over the house whenever she's out of town," Peter remarked.

"Very funny," she smiled. "The day you guys display some maturity and responsibility, I'll stop writing them. ... Oh, and one of the notes, the one on the kitchen table, says you are supposed to phone some fellow named Demetrius? He told me he is a friend of Mr. Winchester's. By the way, how is that lovely old man doing these days?"

Peter walked straight upstairs, making sure his back was to his mom when he replied, (so she wouldn't spot any dishonesty in his answer.)

"He isn't exactly in the best shape," Peter answered. "He's having some heart issues."

"Poor man," his mom replied. "Please give him my regards."

* * *

"Demetrius?" Peter said into the receiver, now sitting on his bed with the door closed. "Everything alright?"

"No, not at all," Demetrius replied, concern evident in his tone. "How soon can you leave your home today? One of us will come and get you. We need to make a plan, and we need to do it now."

Peter's parents were going to be heading out *"at around 5:00,"* which meant they would actually leave sometime between 4:15 and 4:30, since his mom always departed preposterously early.

"Sure, I'll meet you at the park around the corner from my house at a quarter to five," Peter told him.

"Understood," Demetrius answered. "I'll be waiting there."

CHAPTER 9

"What do you mean by *significant movement?*" Peter asked the large group of people now assembled for this emergency meeting at Mr. Winchester's home. "Are you saying a big part of Xavier's fleet is on their way here?"

"Our contacts on Sevlar informed us," Demetrius explained to the group, "that approximately three-and-a-half hours ago, three of Xavier's ships departed from Sevlar. Gauging by the direction they were aiming after launch, they are likely heading to Earth."

"It is important to note that it's only three ships," Torin pointed out. "Nothing too worrisome."

"Unfortunately," Demetrius went on. "Those three ships belong to Xavier's fiercest and most ruthless henchmen. Plus, we have no idea how many troops are packed into each one."

"What do you think their mission is?" Aurora asked. "Possibly they're just doing some scouting?"

"I'm afraid we have no intel on that,"

Demetrius told her. "To be honest, I don't even have a guess."

"We had better get people standing guard here around the clock," Helix (one of Vasilios' most loyal and experienced friends) suggested. "I say we have a team of four stay outside, one on each side of the house. We can work in 2-hour shifts, rotating people so we always have fresh and rested eyes."

"Agreed," Demetrius nodded. "Would you mind taking on the responsibility of organizing that?"

"Not at all," Helix answered, immediately directing four of his men outside for the first shift.

Then Helix got ready to rush to the hotel in Stoneburg to bring back more of his team to help with this task.

CHAPTER 10

Nerves were at a high the entire evening. Every single noise—which was always nothing more than some part of Mr. Winchester's old home rattling in the wind—elicited a sideways glance or an increase in pulse.

* * *

"Peter," Sapphire said when it was almost ten o'clock. "It's too risky for you to return home. You should stay the night."

"Yes, way too risky," Aurora agreed. "For all we know, Xavier's team has already surrounded us, and are just waiting a fair distance back in the shadows where we can't see them."

"Well, we've got a pretty big team here," Torin mentioned, noting that a bunch of their Chronostil friends had arrived as reinforcements. "We should be fine."

Helix had not only brought a sizeable team over, but also sleeping bags for all of them. He even managed to bring enough food to last everyone for at least a few days.

(Mr. Winchester's living room currently looked like an army barracks.)

"Although this is merely my intuition speaking," Helix commented. "I doubt they'll try anything before sunrise, as coordinating an attack at night is complicated. But regardless of my personal opinion, the most important thing is that we don't let our guard down, not even for a minute."

* * *

At midnight, Sapphire demanded that Peter try to get a little shuteye. Peter knew she was right, so he went to Mr. Winchester's bedroom and attempted to fall asleep on the comfy queen-size bed.

* * *

Smash!

A brick had just come flying through the dining room window, causing all those sleeping to jolt awake.

"Away from the windows! Now!" Helix ordered everyone. He then quickly used his communicator to ask the four on guard outside what was happening… but none of them had seen anything.

"This is like a pirate ship shooting one over the front bow," Demetrius remarked. "I think they want us to surrender."

Helix, who had much more battle training and expertise, saw it differently. "Actually," he commented. "I think—"

Smash! Smash!

Two more bricks—one through the kitchen window and one through the living room window—flew in.

"Someone go get Peter and bring him in here!" Sapphire yelled in a panic. "We can't leave him alone in Leonardo's bedroom!"

Helix then reached for his communicator again.

* * *

"I just ordered a large contingent from my team at the hotel to come over immediately," he told everyone. "They should be able to spot where the attackers are while making their way here."

Smash!

...

Smash!

Like a true military leader, Helix knew what they needed to do. He quickly yelled specific orders to his team (and those from Sevlar.) In total, they had twenty-one here who could "fight," hopefully enough to hold off the attacks until more reinforcements arrived.

* * *

"On my command," Helix then said powerfully. Then he waited a few more seconds until everyone was in position. "Everyone ready?"

CHAPTER 11

These 21 "protectors" of Mr. Winchester's home had split up so that they were now positioned at every broken (and unbroken but now open) window, plus the front and back doors.

"Now!" Helix shouted at the top of his lungs.

The whole team of weather gods, at the same instant, shot powerful winds from the small bungalow. Since they were doing this from all different locations in the house, the wind blasts they were sending out protected the home like some sort of *force field,* (similar to something you'd see in a science fiction movie.)

The velocity of their winds was so high that it was sure to blow back anything that Xavier's team hurled their way. (And if they were lucky, they might even be able to force Xavier's men back to a distance where they could no longer attack effectively.)

"Break!" Helix then shouted after they had had their wind blasts going full steam for close to a minute.

...

"Ready again..." he informed his team shortly after. "Now!"

The second blast, equally as strong as the first (but only for a few seconds this time), was basically done to "reassure" Xavier's team that Mr. Winchester's home was currently impenetrable.

The four who had been on watch outside came back in, and Helix explained the next course of action. (He wasn't randomly making up this plan on the fly, as all of these instructions were identical to what Vasilios had trained them to do.)

And since upward of forty more reinforcements were set to arrive from the hotel shortly, they would soon have large enough numbers to effectively fend off all attacks.

* * *

"I love how you are going to include the element of randomness in the defensive strategy," Peter commented to Helix.

"It will keep them confused," Helix smiled. "Which is what we are after. They won't want to attack until they figure out what we are up to, but they never will... That's the beautiful thing about unpredictability."

The *element of randomness* was that all weather gods here—those from both Cronostil and

Sevlar—would, at undetermined intervals, go up to one of the windows and create some type of weather disturbance: be that a wind blast, some pounding hail, a dense fog, or even a tornado. And since they would keep switching from window to window and using different weather attacks each time, this assured no pattern would ever develop.

This scheme was achieved by using a small device which Helix referred to as a "randomizer." He had input the names of all weather gods present, the location of each window, and various weather events. The randomizer was just a simple computer, and its robotic voice perpetually "spat out" commands they could all hear. All everyone had to do was sit and wait until it said his or her name, which window he or she had to go to, and what disturbance to create.

* * *

Since altering the weather required a decent expenditure of physical and mental energy, the whole group of 60 was fairly drained when the sun finally rose the next morning. (Peter and Sapphire had taken on the role of providing everyone with food and beverages all night. And Torin was monitoring everyone closely, advising those who looked exhausted to take breaks.)

* * *

Dawn brought the team a new level of comfort, as the sun meant that attacking from close range was next to impossible now. Helix reconfigured the randomizer to emit orders less frequently, which would help his already-tired group conserve as much energy as possible, (as this battle was far from over...)

* * *

Peter, Demetrius, Aurora, Cynthia, Torin, and Maximilian went to Mr. Winchester's bedroom so they could discuss their current predicament, and decide on what they should (or shouldn't) do next. Cynthia and Maximilian were standing by the broken window. (It was always better to be safe than sorry, right?)

"We can't wait any longer," Maximilian commented. "If we just sit here, Xavier will eventually send more troops until he overwhelms our defenses."

"I agree," Demetrius nodded. "Peter, are we currently ready to proceed?"

"N... no, not really," Peter replied, wishing he had some way to communicate with Mr. Winchester. "I mean, we need Zoltan in order to enact this plan. And that can't happen until Mr. Winchester gets his *task* done first."

Demetrius cracked a bit of a smile. "Leonardo, more than anyone," he said, "can be counted on to accomplish whatever is required of him. He's also unbelievably sly and resourceful. I guarantee he knows that Xavier has sent ships to Earth. Whatever it is you have instructed Leonardo to do, he'll get it done. Let's move forward under the assumption that his task is almost complete."

"Um... okay," Peter said, unfortunately not sharing in Demetrius' confidence. "Then first I need to get Neil, Nik, Brad, Sophia, and Claire over here, right away."

"Torin, Cynthia, Aurora," Demetrius told them. "You three help Peter collect his team."

"Wouldn't it be less conspicuous if Brad just drove them all here? Torin suggested.

"What do you think, Peter?" Demetrius replied, deferring this decision.

"Let's go in those little tornado things," Peter smiled. "The best form of transit I've ever used."

"Just make sure you triple-check that no civilians see you doing this," Demetrius advised. "We don't want the people of Earth to think they are being attacked by aliens or something silly like that."

CHAPTER 12

Back on Axon, the medical team in charge of Mr. Winchester's care was relieved (and a little bewildered...)

After running more scans than they could count (using technology so advanced that it made Earth's hospitals look archaic), the skilled doctors and technicians were unable to find anything "wrong" with the old man.

Of course, his aged body was nowhere near that of a healthy young person, but every single exam they did produced results in the normal range. The doctors accredited this to the active lifestyle he had adopted after his heart surgery. (So all those early morning walks were paying off!)

The closest they could get to providing a clinical diagnosis about why he had suddenly passed out while with Peter was this: *vasovagal syncope...* Basically, this is a poorly understood phenomenon where one's brain suddenly thinks it's being deprived of necessary blood. In order to quickly get as much blood as possible to the brain, the mind *forces* unconsciousness, thus the person falls over. Once flat on the ground, blood is no longer required to battle against gravity, and can immediately rush to one's brain.

And the wobbly/weird/dizzy feeling after his fall had likely been from a concussion caused by the impact on his head.

* * *

One morning (less than two weeks after the fall), Dradzig Hospital's chief doctor had come in to deliver some wonderful news to Mr. Winchester: He was being given a clean bill of health, with permission to return to Earth.

Mr. Winchester, however, knew he had something he needed to accomplish first... a near-impossible mission given to him by Peter in the form of a coded note in his pocket.

Dear Leonardo,

We are heading back to Earth. The doctors here will nurse you back to health.

Please be kind and cooperative. Remember, they are providing this medical treatment for free!

(Don't be rude and disrespectful, like

some of your former students...)

Take care,

Peter

Peter had done a reasonably good job writing this note in a way that wouldn't cause Quill (or any of the doctors) to get suspicious, as it appeared to be nothing more than a polite message encouraging his elderly friend to trust the medical professionals.

But Mr. Winchester knew there was more to the note than that! The instant he saw the note was titled "Leonardo" (a name Peter had NEVER called him by), he was positive his young friend was informing him of something important.

* * *

"Oh, Peter," Mr. Winchester had chuckled while reading the note for the first time (the day after he had been admitted.) "This is quite a task you have for me..."

HI READER!
ANY GUESS AT WHAT TASK PETER HAS GIVEN TO MR. WINCHESTER?
HERE'S A HINT: THE SECRET MESSAGE IS HIDDEN IN THE SECOND HALF OF THE NOTE!

It didn't even take Mr. Winchester five minutes to decipher the mission he had been assigned.

"Peter must have written this in a hurry," Mr. Winchester had said to himself. "He used a very simple trick to call my attention to the first important word... he used an exclamation mark."

free!

"And then he used brackets to *hint at* the second word," Mr. Winchester had said to himself. "Implying that I'd have to figure that one out for myself."

(Don't be rude and disrespectful, like some of your former students...)

"Peter certainly knows which one of my students was the biggest troublemaker," Mr. Winchester had thought. "None other than the one I had to follow to Earth to babysit... Zoltan. Put those two words together, and what do I get?"

Free Zoltan

"But now comes the hard part," he had said, shaking his head. "As I know absolutely nothing about the specifics... Free Zoltan from where? From whom? From what?"

CHAPTER 13

Peter knew his friends' parents might consider
calling the police if some stranger (wearing a
cloak!) rang the doorbell at half past six on a
Saturday morning asking for their child by name.
Therefore, the three weather gods hid out of sight
at the end of each block as Peter went up to Nicola,
Claire, and Neil's front doors.

These three conversations were all extremely
short, as Peter's friends knew this day was coming
sooner or later, (and all three had prepared their
backpacks ages ago, just in case.) The only thing
they needed to do this morning was change into
appropriate clothes, grab comfortable shoes and a
light jacket, and tell a parent they were heading
out for the day with Peter. (Everyone's parents
considered Peter a "wonderful little angel," so they
happily waved goodbye and told their son or
daughter to enjoy their day with him.)

* * *

"Peter," Torin suggested before departing for

their final pick-up spot: Peter's house. "Why don't Cynthia and Aurora fly these three back to Mr. Winchester's? They can be brought up to speed while we go fetch Brad and Sophia."

"Sounds good," Peter agreed. "See you guys soon."

* * *

Peter went to his front door and twisted the handle without putting in his key to unlock it, just like he would do when intentionally leaving it unlocked to play basketball in their driveway.

Hmm... it wasn't locked today...

"Looks like Brad or Soph forgot to read the note," Peter laughed while walking in and taking the *Lock the deadbolt before bed'* note off the inside of the door. "But hey, I probably would have forgotten, too."

"Brad! Soph!" Peter yelled, going up two steps at a time to the second floor. "Wake up! We gotta go! Xavier is up to something!"

Sophia was a pretty light sleeper, so Peter expected his sister to exit her room shortly. But Bradley (who could sleep through a rock concert!) would need more prodding to awaken.

"C'mon, Brad!" Peter yelled, opening Bradley's bedroom door." Get your butt out of—"

But Bradley was not in his room...

"Drat, he must have track practice this morning," Peter commented. He then knocked on his sister's door twice before opening it. "Soph... you awake yet?" he said.

No reply...

"Soph?" he asked while cracking the door open a few inches. "You in there?"

His sister wasn't at home either...

"Peter!" Torin called from downstairs. "Think she might have stayed over at a friend's house?"

"Yeah, probably," Peter replied. "Go check the kitchen table, she would have left me a note if she did."

* * *

When Peter got to the kitchen, he saw Torin holding a sheet of paper in one hand and a small device in the other.

"You had better sit down," Torin said, handing Peter the messily written note.

Hello Peter!

Our brick bombardment at Mr. Winchester's provided a wonderful distraction, just like we had planned!

That made it so easy to come here and abduct your family!

We only got two though... Seems your parents are out of town...

Well, I suppose two is enough, now isn't it?

Take the small communicator we left on the table. When you are ready, press the button, and we will inform you of the location for the exchange.

What exchange, you ask? Well, your brother and sister for the amulet, of course!

You will also notice that a 24-hour countdown has already started on the communicator. It began counting the instant we finished writing this note. If you don't contact us before the time runs out, then you can kiss your brother and sister goodbye.

Oh, it feels so good to have the upper hand!

It was a good thing that Peter had taken Torin's

advice to sit down, as he instantly felt a wave of nausea flow over him. His whole body seemed to be emitting a cold sweat, a tell-tale sign he was in complete "fight or flight" mode.

"Timer's showing about seventeen hours to go," Torin said, unsure of what comment might help calm Peter down a little. "That means they were here at about midnight."

"I should have seen this coming," Peter scolded himself. "I mean, it was so obvious, a kidnapping…"

"Don't beat yourself up, Peter," Torin said, patting Peter's shoulder. "Let's just focus on how to proceed from here."

"How to *proceed!?*" Peter blurted out, shocked by the lack of sympathy in that advice. "You make it sound like Brad and Soph are just collateral damage."

"That's not what I meant, and you know it," Torin said back. "And look at it this way: If he harms either of them, he knows we won't hand over the amulet. He's bluffing."

Peter shook his head and stormed out of the house.

* * *

Torin followed about twenty meters behind Peter (who was speed-walking through the subdivision, seemingly heading nowhere.) He had tried calling to Peter twice, but was ignored both times, so he figured all he could do for now was stay close behind and wait.

Eventually, Peter would come to his senses and take control of the situation again. (Or at least that's what Torin was hoping...)

CHAPTER 14

Torin knew he had to exercise patience with his panicking and overwhelmed friend, but after ten minutes of senselessly following Peter, he started to feel a little agitated.

"I have to give him a few more minutes," Torin told himself. "Poor kid has a lot on his shoulders. And his mind."

Since Peter was currently in *paranoid overdrive,* (and he had not consciously chosen where to head), his body seemed to be moving in autopilot. For some reason, he was using the exact same route he took to go to school every morning.

"This is almost the same spot I ran into that freaky Neil look-alike," Peter mumbled to himself. Then he giggled a bit while thinking of statistical probabilities. "I mean, odds are there might be a few others that look like him in the country. But c'mon, a Neil replica in the same small town?"

* * *

Then something *clicked* in Peter's mind!

Torin noticed that his friend's pace had suddenly slowed down. And a few seconds later, Peter had completely stopped walking.

"That's more like it," Torin smiled to himself. "I believe we are back in business."

Peter then turned around and ran toward Torin. "I've got a plan!" he yelled. "Fly me back to Mr. Winchester's as fast as you can! I've gotta contact Zoltan!"

"Your wish is my command," Torin smiled, conjuring up a twister for the two of them. "Be there in a jiffy."

CHAPTER 15

"Let me get this straight," Zoltan said into his communicator, now talking to Peter about this plan. "You want me to get the Sevlarian government to use their facial recognition software system to find someone who looks exactly like Xavier's daughter?"

"Precisely," Peter replied. "But we can't *sell her* as being Bridget unless we also find a way to cut off communication between Xavier and the real Bridget. You told me a few weeks ago she was on another planet somewhere training her skills, right?"

"Yes, and she's still there," Zoltan told him. "And since our intel knows where that planet is, we could, in theory, send a ship to orbit it and interfere with the communication channel." Zoltan paused to contemplate this two-part scheme a little bit more. "With some help from a friend I have at planetary security here, plus the blessing and approval from Cygnus, the lead weather god who has been assisting me, we should be able to get the facial recognition software up and running right away."

"Fantastic," Peter replied, finally sensing a turn of the tide. "But how long do you think it will take to complete all of that?"

"I can't say," Zoltan told Peter. "But the Sevlarian government knows the awful predicament their planet is currently in. They will surely make this *top priority.*"

"We've got less than sixteen hours before I have to contact Xavier's group," Peter explained. "Can you do it by then?"

"Yikes, that's a tough timeline to meet," Zoltan answered. Then he paused again, remembering something his friend at planetary security had told him in the past... "But if Cygnus evokes a state of emergency here, then all personnel will drop what they are doing to work on this. Alright, I'll make sure it's done before then, you have my word."

"Awesome," Peter said back. "Keep me posted."

* * *

Although Peter was being bombarded with questions, (some from his friends, some from Cynthia and Torin, plus a couple from Demetrius), he ignored them all and focused on his notebook.

He reread the tasks currently being worked on: The one he had just spoken to Zoltan about, and the extremely difficult one in Mr. Winchester's hands…

Then he flipped the page and stared at the one "unknown" yet to be answered:

Find a suitable site for this showdown.

Earth would provide an unfair advantage for Peter's team, and Sevlar would benefit Xavier, so Peter considered both of those planets off-limits.

"Demetrius," Peter said, asking the old man to come outside with him to speak where it was a little quieter. "How much do you know about Axon?"

"A fair bit," Demetrius replied. "Well, I'm sure old age has robbed me of some of the fine details, but the bulk of it is still up in my head somewhere… What specifically are you interested in?"

* * *

After listening to Peter outline the specifics of what type of site he hoped existed on Axon, Demetrius provided a reply that was even better than Peter had expected.

"Axons have always been very competitive, even amongst themselves," he told Peter. "In fact, ages ago, they created a *competition zone* of sorts, which allows the best of the best to go head-to-head against each other, to determine who is the better puzzler."

"And you're SURE that the rock composition at

that location renders everyone completely powerless?" Peter asked, needing confirmation of this important point.

"The site was chosen specifically for that reason," Demetrius explained. "They needed a place where one's mind was the only thing that could be tested."

"Let's sit down," Peter said, motioning for Demetrius to head over to the bench.

Peter then got out his paper and pencil. "Now tell me everything you know about this head-to-head puzzle-off site on Axon," he said. "And I mean EVERYTHING!"

CHAPTER 16

It didn't take Mr. Winchester long to admit that he couldn't accomplish what was required of him without some form of help...

(He had surreptitiously begun an investigation into what the meaning of *'Free Zoltan'* was. And the first thing he had tried was to casually ask Quill if Zoltan and Klaron had made it back to Earth safely.)

Quill, not suspecting anything, updated Mr. Winchester on how those two were currently "trapped" on Sevlar (because of the tracking devices made by the Axon government.) Quill also explained how the wristbands worked: and that trying to tamper with them would cause the wearer to be injected with poison.

Despite his reservations about what trouble could spawn by confiding in someone here, Mr. Winchester still elected to have a long and serious chat with Quill.

* * *

"Leonardo," Quill told him after hearing the old man explain that Peter had run off with BOTH amulets. "I am, well, shocked... I would never have taken you for the type to tell lies."

"I'm not proud of it either," Mr. Winchester replied. "But as you can understand, we are ALL doomed if Xavier gets too strong."

"I agree with you there," Quill said next. "But the Axon government will just laugh at you if you tell them the story about Xavier and all the evil things he's up to. ... We will have to navigate our way through everything secretly."

"By the nuance in your comment," Mr. Winchester smiled. "I take it you have enough people on the inside here to help us get this done?"

Quill pulled out his communicator. "I'm calling my close friend Realgar right now," he said. "He works in prison technology, so hopefully he'll be able to help us figure out how to get that locator device off Zoltan's wrist without killing him."

"But if Realgar is caught digging into things above his level of clearance," Mr. Winchester mentioned. "Won't that spur an investigation? Which could potentially expose the fact that Axon has been infiltrated by you and your ancestors for so long?"

"It is a huge risk," Quill admitted. "But all things considered, doing nothing would be much, much riskier."

CHAPTER 17

"In a nutshell," Demetrius said, beginning a long explanation of the site to Peter. "The competition zone, which is called *Dorado,* was designed for two teams to compete against each other head-to-head. They are both trying to solve the same series of puzzles, at the same time, in adjacent chambers. Since they aren't in the same room, they can't see or hear each other."

"Cool," Peter nodded, kind of wishing this was something he could do for fun instead of to save the world... "How many people per team? And how many puzzles are there?"

"Sorry, but I don't know those specifics," he admitted.

"Is time a factor?" Peter asked next. "Is it also a race?"

"Oh, yes indeed," Demetrius went on. "But there is one important thing I should point out: If either team is unable to solve even one of the puzzles, then that team automatically loses the entire competition."

"Ah," Peter nodded. "So, if you try to go too quickly and botch something up, you're toast."

"Exactly," Demetrius said. "And as a way to keep the opposition aware of your team's progress, both teams are given a small device, which is worn on the wrist of each team's captain. A green light turns on when the other team completes a challenge successfully."

"Intriguing," Peter smiled. "Then you always know whether you're in the lead or not."

"Yes, I suspect that was added to amplify the level of competition," Demetrius commented.

* * *

Peter looked down at his long list of notes. "There is one thing that unnerves me a little," he told Demetrius. "I'm worried about the fact that we don't have Bradley and Sophia on our team this time."

"But with you and your friends, plus Zoltan," Demetrius mentioned, "that's five, right? Why not add Max and Cynthia? They are superb puzzlers."

"Because they are needed for a separate part of my plan," Peter answered. "Plus, having them with me, where they'd be completely powerless, is too risky."

Neil unexpectedly popped his head outside. "Dudes, keep me in the loop here," he laughed. "What's cookin'?"

"Peter was just mentioning that there aren't

enough of you and your friends this time," Demetrius told Neil. "Because of what happened to Bradley and Sophia."

"Petey," Neil said, jokingly slapping his friend's back. "Get Freddy in on this, man! We both know he's mega-smart."

"Freddy?" Demetrius asked curiously. "Who's that?"

"He's a new kid at school, and amazingly clever," Peter told Demetrius. "He and his sister have even published a book filled with cool puzzles."

"Let's bring her along too!" Neil exclaimed.

"Peter," Demetrius said calmly. "This decision is ultimately up to you. But based on your track record when it comes to choosing friends and teammates, I think these two might be beneficial to have on our side, especially after hearing they are both so intrigued by puzzles."

* * *

A minute later, Neil (who had just run back inside and returned with Cynthia and Torin) said, "I'm coming to help with the *convincing,* Pete. Here's your jacket."

Torin and Cynthia got their twisters going.

"Sorry to be so bossy," Neil said to his friend.

"Actually, thanks," Peter replied, getting ready to lift off with Torin. "I never would have thought of that if you hadn't said something. Just make sure to keep your skills of persuasion going when we get to Freddy's place."

"No problem," Neil laughed. "You leave the smooth-talkin' to the Neilster!"

CHAPTER 18

Very little "convincing" was needed to get Frederick and Valerie on board. (A little display of weather-altering skills by Torin and Cynthia was more than enough to make them realize that everything was very real...)

But the two *new recruits* had opposite reactions after being informed they were about to be flown (in tornados!) to Mr. Winchester's home.

"Pete," Valerie said to him nervously. "I'm super afraid of heights. I don't think I can do this."

Frederick and Neil were already up in the air in Cynthia's twister. Frederick was so astonished by what was happening that he could barely contain his excitement.

"It's like walking on air!" he yelled down to his sister. "It's not scary at all, trust me!"

Peter could see how pale Valerie's face was. (But even though she was so terrified, she still looked stunning...)

He took her hands. (And for the first time in his

life, his palms were NOT sweating profusely!) "I've got you," he told her supportively. "Don't worry."

Valerie closed her eyes and took a deep breath. Then she squeezed Peter's hands so hard that he could see his fingertips starting to go purple.

"Don't you dare let go of me," she said loudly to Peter. "And please make sure he flies this thing very, very slowly."

* * *

Cynthia started flying Neil and Frederick back at a fast pace, and Torin opted to go much slower with Peter and Valerie.

About ten seconds after they started their flight, Valerie had been so afraid that she switched from grabbing Peter's hands to wrapping both her arms around him. The left side of her face was pressed up against Peter's, and he worried a bit about whether his prickly whiskers were irritating her. (He really regretted not shaving this morning!)

Peter made sure to talk during the entire *flight,* hoping that rattling on about weather god history might distract her mind a little.

* * *

When Torin's group finally arrived—a good ten minutes after Cynthia's—Frederick had already met the bulk of those at Mr. Winchester's home.

"The eagle has landed," Neil announced when Peter and Valerie's feet touched the grass.

Valerie opened her eyes, but she didn't let go of Peter right away.

"I think I just aged ten years in the last ten minutes," she commented, finally breathing a sigh of relief. Peter could feel her heart pounding rapidly against his chest.

"Let me introduce you to everyone," Peter told her, waiting patiently until she was comfortable enough to relax her hold on him.

CHAPTER 19

Less than two hours after contacting Realgar to ask him more about the locator bracelet on Zoltan's wrist, Quill received a short (but slightly discomforting) reply.

"Leonardo," he said, preparing to explain the contents of the massage. "I have some good news and some bad news."

"Well, I always like the good first," the old man smiled.

"Realgar managed to find a loophole in the locking mechanism," Quill explained. "Which means we should be able to unlock Zoltan's bracelet."

"Wonderful," Mr. Winchester smiled. "Now let me take a stab at the bad news here... Perhaps you are about to inform me that there is still a small chance of the poison accidentally being injected into his wrist while we attempt to take it off?"

"Nice try, but not even close," Quill went on.

"The caveat is this: although the bracelet can be unlocked, which will allow us to remove it from Zoltan's wrist, it must be relocked again within ten seconds."

"Ah," Mr. Winchester nodded. "And I suppose the device itself would notice if we attached it to a lamppost or tree limb or something like that."

"Indeed, it would," Quill told Mr. Winchester. "It'll have to go on someone else's wrist. And then that person will have to remain on Sevlar."

...

"And the instant we do the bracelet transfer," Quill continued. "The Axon government will be notified of a possible malfunction. They'll likely then send a team to Sevlar to investigate."

Mr. Winchester started chuckling... "Guess I had better practice up on my *hiding,* then," he mentioned. "For the upcoming *hide-and-seek marathon* I'm about to embark on."

"You're not suggesting we put the locator bracelet on YOUR wrist, are you?" Quill asked in shock. "We can surely find someone stronger and younger and—"

"I'm not putting this dangerous task in anyone else's hands," Mr. Winchester said with conviction. Then he grinned a little. "Or *on anyone else's wrist,* which I suppose would be a more accurate description. Ha ha."

"Understood," Quill nodded, figuring that no amount of persuasion would change the stubborn old man's mind. "When shall we head to Sevlar?"

"Immediately," Mr. Winchester answered. "Oh, and I have another favor to ask."

"Which is…?" Quill inquired.

"I need to quickly borrow the communicator you use to send messages to Peter," Mr. Winchester told him. "They'll want to know I'm about to head to Sevlar."

"This new device is a bit tricky to operate," Quill said, placing it down on the table. "After I press this, just dictate your message. Everything you say will automatically be picked up and written into sentences here. Then we just double-check that nothing is missing, and hit *SEND.*"

"Quite the technology," Mr. Winchester laughed. "Way beyond my time."

CHAPTER 20

"Peter!" Sapphire called, coming out to the front porch. "We've just received another message from Axon. And believe it or not, this one's from Leonardo!"

"Really!?" Peter replied excitedly. "What does it say?"

"Here," she said, passing him the communicator. "I'll let you read it for yourself."

> *I'm on my way to Sevlar now, and have found out how to safely remove Zoltan's wristband.*
>
> *Please give my regards to everyone,*
>
> *Leonardo*

"Yes!" Peter cheered.

"I told you that crafty devil would get it done," Demetrius smiled. "That man has never failed at anything."

* * *

Everyone then packed into Mr. Winchester's living room, and Peter began outlining the specifics of the multi-phase plan they were about to put into action.

"But we still haven't received word from Zoltan about whether or not he managed to find a Bridget look-alike," Maximilian pointed out.

"True," Peter admitted. "But he'll find one, and probably fairly soon. Um… does anyone else have any concerns?"

"Concerns…? Not really," Frederick said, hand raised like a schoolkid. "But if you are also taking questions, then I have a fairly long list of ones I'd like answered."

Neil walked over and put his arm playfully on Frederick's shoulder. "Dude," he commented, laughing. "You are a total clone of Pete. He also hates it when he doesn't know every last little detail."

"While Torin gets a portion of our fleet ready to depart," Peter told Frederick. "I'll sit down with you and Val and answer everything as best as I can."

"Can't wait," Valerie smiled, giving Peter a wink (that no one else spotted.)

(Hold on… What exactly was that wink for? Does Valerie have a crush on Peter?? … No way… But, come to think of it, she sure did hold him close during their tornado ride...)

Peter! Stop letting yourself get distracted!!

CHAPTER 21

The first part of Peter's plan was going to be carried out solely by a large contingent from Chronostil, primarily because of their high level of tactical training and expertise.

Twenty ships from Chronostil, with a total of sixty-four people on board (roughly half of their total numbers), were currently on their way to Sevlar. And thanks to intel supplied by Zoltan over the past few weeks, they knew where the majority of Xavier's troops were training, plus the spots where most of their ships were being stored. They didn't, unfortunately, know where Xavier was currently hiding out, though...

The other half of the Chronostil crew, the ones remaining on Earth, were tasked with securing Mr. Winchester's home every minute, night and day. They were going to be working in rotations, ensuring that everyone got at least a reasonable amount of rest.

* * *

"I've got some news," Peter told Zoltan when he got through to him on the communicator. "Two things, in fact. One: a large group from Chronostil is heading to Sevlar right now, to carry out the mission I explained before. And two: Mr. Winchester found out how to remove your stupid bracelet. He's on his way to rendezvous with you."

"Well, speaking of good updates," Zoltan said back. "I have some as well. We have found someone who is a spitting image of Bridget. Her name's Jakayla, and luckily she lives here in the capital. Cygnus has just spoken to her, and she has agreed to help. Plus, the team of technicians with the communication jamming device is now orbiting the planet where Bridget is doing her training. They will soon get to work setting it up to cut off communications between her and her father."

* * *

"All captains, ready yourselves," Helix (the Chronostil representative running the show for today's onslaught) told the captains of the other nineteen ships as they orbited Sevlar.

All nineteen of those captains knew their roles today, which they had rehearsed numerous times back on Earth. Of course, there would be some *surprises* and *unknowns,* the biggest one being the level of resistance they'd be met with after initiating this attack.

They were going to target the large hangar

where they knew Xavier stored at least half of his fleet. There would, no doubt, be some crew there as well, but not nearly as many as there would be if they were to go after one of the training locations or dormitories.

"Engage!" Helix instructed the captains. "Head down, in formation, at full speed... And await my next command." (Helix was going to remain in orbit, so he could alter the plan as necessary to account for any unexpected developments or complications.)

* * *

Thirty seconds after they entered the atmosphere, Helix gave them their next instruction. "Turn on your hologram projectors," he ordered all captains.

All of their ships were equipped with two sets of amazing high-tech projectors, one starboard and one aft. Each one was configured to project a realistic (and properly sized) 3-D image of a ship. So, to the security team waiting at the hangar, it looked like a huge fleet of 57 (19 real ships plus 38 holograms) was headed their way!

"Beautiful," Helix commented to himself. "That should get them shaking in their boots."

* * *

Since all Chronostil vessels were not equipped with external weaponry, they couldn't do any actual *attacking* until they had landed and exited their ships.

They set down in a huge, half-circle formation in front of the hangar, with all 19 ships (and the 38 fake ships being projected) facing the hangar itself.

The captain of each ship had to remain inside at the controls, but all others exited and began the roles they had rehearsed. Eighteen worked together to make a massive tornado, which they hoped would rip the hangar (and some of the ships inside) to shreds. Twelve (who were now standing on the tops of the ships) were waiting to send wind blasts at all evil weather gods they saw emerging from the facility. And twelve more, also standing on the ships, were waiting to defend against attacks they knew were surely coming.

* * *

The instant Helix, still hovering in orbit, got word that those on the surface had conjured up a powerful tornado, he pressed the dark blue button on his control panel. This released a set of experimental drones from his hull. These cool devices had only been developed a few years earlier by a group of young engineers.

The 25 1-meter-wide flying drones were not equipped with weapons or surveillance, because they had a completely different purpose. Each one was fitted with a hologram projector, so when Helix flicked the switch to turn those on, it looked like 25 full-sized ships were dive-bombing Sevlar. And all 25 were heading to perform a flyby at one of the big dormitories where a large chunk of Xavier's team lived and trained.

"If I can play this just right," Helix said to himself. "They'll never figure out these things aren't real."

* * *

The ever-growing tornado was doing a great job of peeling away pieces of the big hangar's walls and roof. If they could maintain its current size and speed, they stood a good chance of turning at least a few ships into piles of useless, bent metal.

But before that could happen, the resistance they were expecting emerged. Xavier's men appeared to come from a few sets of doors on the floor of the hangar, likely underground lodging built to keep them safe from bomb attacks.

The crew from Chronostil had another technological advantage today: each was wearing a set of *battle goggles*, which could quickly recognize and indicate the exact locations of all attackers by sensing their body heat. And since Xavier's men were coming from one of six doors in the floor, the wind blasts they were hitting them with after exiting were doing their job beautifully.

"Come on, Xavier..." Helix said to himself. "Show yourself..."

CHAPTER 22

"More good news," Zoltan told Peter through the communicator a while later. "The team employing the jamming device has it fully operational. If Xavier tries to contact Bridget, all he'll get is noisy static."

"Awesome," Peer replied, pleased to see how piece after piece of this puzzle was finally falling in place.

"And hold on a second," Zoltan said before Peter hung up. "I have someone here who can't wait to say hello."

"Peter!" Mr. Winchester bellowed cheerfully into the communicator. "You sure weren't gonna let little old me get any rest, were you?"

"Mr. Winchester!" Peter said back, laughing. "C'mon, you would have been bored to tears if I left you on Axon with nothing to occupy your mind."

"You might be right," Mr. Winchester agreed, still laughing away. "Anyway, let's save the chitchat for later. I'm about to remove Zoltan's locator bracelet, and place it on my own wrist."

"On YOUR wrist?" Peter asked, surprised. "Why would you—"

"There's no time for me to go into the technical details," Mr. Winchester told his friend.

"But—" Peter tried to say.

"I'm putting the communicator on the table for a minute while I do this," Mr. Winchester said, not allowing Peter to finish his question.

...

"Done," Mr. Winchester said thirty seconds later. "I am now the not-so-proud owner of a poison-filled wristband."

"Lucky you," Zoltan commented in jest, loud enough for Peter to hear, too.

"Zoltan is now officially a free man," Mr. Winchester said next. "Which means you can move onto the next phase of the plan."

Peter, although a little worried about his elderly friend, forced out a small laugh. "You took the words right out of my mouth," he told his mentor. "Now you just stay put on Sevlar while Zoltan and I take care of Xavier once and for all."

"I like the sound of that," Mr. Winchester replied. "I think I'm going to pour myself a cup of aberleaf tea as soon as we finish this call. I haven't smelled that lovely aroma in ages..."

CHAPTER 23

"Xavier's on the move!" Helix announced for all to hear. "His ship and five others have just launched from some remote island in the middle of The Larimar Ocean!"

"I guess that's where he has been hiding," Demetrius—whose communicator was tuned in to pick up all chatter between Helix and his team—remarked.

"Think they're heading to Earth?" Maximilian pondered, wanting to hear others' opinions as well. "Should we beef up protection here?"

"I doubt they would launch an attack with only five or six ships," Demetrius replied. "I think he's doing just what Peter expected him to do: fleeing Sevlar out of fear for his safety."

"Helix," Peter then said into the communicator. "You know what to do next."

"We will begin immediately," Helix said back.

Helix had always considered the use of deception a big key to success in any battle. Today, more than ever, he was depending on it.

"All captains," he instructed the 19 down on Axon. "Have your men get started now. And do your best to *sell this...*"

The team executed this well-rehearsed ruse, which would only be convincing if everyone performed their roles to perfection: Those creating the giant tornado reduced its size significantly, meaning Xavier's men wouldn't lose their footing anymore. The group tasked with sending wind blasts to knock down every new evil weather god who emerged from one of the doors also intentionally began "missing their marks."

Timing was crucial here. Whenever one of Xavier's men sent a lightning bolt at one of the Chronostil ships, a list of things had to happen in rapid succession... (All captains were waiting eagle-eyed to see when a lightning blast was sent at one of the holograms their ship was projecting.) When that happened, they were to immediately relay that information to Soren and Aurelius, who were hiding behind the ships, out of sight.

Each time Soren received that info, he "added" his own lightning to it, making the resulting explosion much bigger than it would have been.

And Aurelius then made a sudden cloud of smoke.

As soon as the smoke engulfed the entire hologram, the captain at the controls pushed a button to change the hologram from its current one to a ship in ruins.

(Xavier's team now thought it was knocking off the ships one by one, but all they were doing was receiving a high-tech, pre-prepared light show!)

* * *

"Only five more hologram projections left," Helix told his team about ten minutes after starting this scheme. "Prepare to launch immediately after that happens."

* * *

"That was number 38!" Helix announced as the last of the 38 holograms was changed to project a mangled vessel. "Everyone back on your ships, now!"

This would have usually provided an opportunity for Xavier's men to attack relentlessly, but the timely arrival of the twenty-five drones (which looked like full-size ships) would ensure that didn't happen.

The drones then released what looked like a haphazard and disorganized "fireworks display." Hundreds of lights popped and flashed in all directions, making it impossible for Xavier's troops to see the Chronostil fleet through the smoky, flashing mess. Plus, the fireworks also contained ion-charged particles, which would dissipate or alter Xavier's men's attempts to randomly shoot lightening through the smoke.

* * *

A minute or two later, when the smoke had cleared, the whole fleet from Chronostil was flying safely away. And the twenty-five drones (still emitting their "full-sized ship" holograms), followed right behind.

This plan was going well! (At least, so far...)

CHAPTER 24

Peter had informed Zoltan where to rendezvous with him and the others who were currently on their way from Earth. (They couldn't risk entering Axon's atmosphere in their own ships today, as that would trigger an alert: meaning an Axon security team would come to investigate...)

"I'm waiting in orbit, directly above Axon's North Pole," Zoltan said though his ship's communicator to Torin (who was piloting the ship with Peter and his team.) "And Jakayla, the Sevlarian girl who will be posing as Bridget, is here with me. Oh, and Quill is in his vessel, just next to mine. We'll wait for you to arrive before boarding his ship."

"We should be there in about twenty-five minutes," Torin told Zoltan. "Just sit tight."

* * *

The team Torin was flying consisted of himself, Neil, Peter, Nicola, Claire, Frederick, Valerie, and Aurora. Peter had originally wanted to bring a few more weather gods along, but ultimately decided against it, as that would have left Earth more exposed to Xavier's forces.

Torin's assignment was to remain aboard the vessel the whole time, and Aurora would take the helm of Zoltan's ship while Zoltan went down to Axon. They'd be orbiting Axon, ready to dart to the surface if an emergency came up.

Getting from one vessel to another in the vacuum of space required the ships to position themselves close together, and then deploy (and attach) to one another using a crawl-size tube. (There was no such thing as the teleporters or transporters seen on sci-fi TV shows... Too bad, as that would have made this a lot easier!)

***

After the docking maneuvers were complete, everyone (other than Torin and Aurora) moved to Quill's ship, which could easily land on Axon without raising suspicion, since it was not a foreign vessel.

"Zoltan!" Peter yelled, running over to hug his friend. "Man, it's good to see you!"

"You as well!" Zoltan said back. "And I see a couple of new faces here."

"Oh, yeah," Peter replied, a little embarrassed that he had forgotten to do the introductions. "My new friends, and our new teammates, Freddy and Val."

"A pleasure to meet you both," Zoltan said,

politely shaking their hands. "A friend of Peter's is a friend of mine."

Zoltan then took a minute to introduce Jakayla. She certainly was the spitting image of Bridget: The only thing that didn't match perfectly was her voice, as this young woman's tone was a fair bit higher. (They would have to make sure she never spoke today.)

"All right, sit down and strap on your seat belts," Quill instructed everyone on board. "I'm taking us to Dorado, the competition site. It's in a pretty hard-to-get-to, secretive location, deep in a mountain range. This ride might get a little bumpy..."

Upon hearing that remark, Valerie made sure she was sitting next to Peter. And before he knew it, she was squeezing his right hand, very hard.

CHAPTER 25

Quill's choice of the phrase *'a little bumpy'* was an understatement, to say the least; The ship shook around so much that almost everyone on board was dizzy with motion sickness when they finally arrived at the spot high up in the mountains. (When the turbulence had started to get bad, Quill informed everyone that their seats had *barf bags* in the side pockets. Thankfully no one had to use one, but Valerie had come very close...)

* * *

"Pete," Valerie said to him, relieved that the ship was finally on solid ground. "Please promise me I will never have to go through that again."

"Um," Peter hesitated, looking at the purple fingers on his right hand. "But, uh... we'll have to take off from here again later."

"Oh, true," she sighed... But then she seemed to perk up a little and leaned in close to Peter's ear. "I will say this though," she whispered to him. "You were totally impressing me until you started making me fly here and there..." She then winked while letting go of his hand.

Before exiting Quill's vessel, they needed to get a message to Xavier, pretending that they had kidnapped his daughter. Xavier was surely in a state of panic after the attack on the hangar, and had likely already tried (unsuccessfully, thanks to the jamming device) to contact Bridget to make sure she was safe.

"I hate to ask you to do this," Peter said to Jakayla. "But I think it's best if we tape your mouth shut. That way, if Xavier asks you something, you won't have to voice a reply."

"I'm happy to cooperate in any way you like," Jakayla told Peter. "Xavier is *evil* in its worst form, and he must be stopped. If gagging me gives us a better chance, then go for it."

They carefully taped her mouth shut, and also tied her hands behind her back. Then they had her sit down on one of the seats. Everyone (other than Quill, who would operate the camera) stood beside or behind her, with stone cold expressions on their faces.

"This message will broadcast on Sevlar's emergency frequency, which Xavier is certainly hooked into," Quill said. "Just give me the word when you are ready to start."

...

"Begin broadcasting," Peter told Quill, giving him a thumbs-up sign.

"Tit for tat," Peter said, angrily starting the speech Xavier would be watching. "Hard to believe you were so foolish as to leave your daughter open to be kidnapped..."

...

"I believe we are both in a similar predicament now," Peter went on. "You have my brother and sister, and we have your daughter. Here's how we are going to resolve this, and ALL of our differences, once and for all. Zoltan, show him the stone."

Zoltan removed the new amulet from his pocket and took it a few steps closer to the camera.

"This whole ridiculous ordeal is happening because of this silly rock." Peter continued. "Which you seem to be prepared to go to any means to acquire.

"Oh, but let me tell you one thing first: If my brother or sister is harmed in any way, you'll never see this amulet. Plus, you can forget a reunion with your lovely Bridget.

"So, let's settle this stalemate... Why? Well, because I am sick and tired of all this nonsense, and more than anything I just want to return to a normal life back on Earth.

"Bring a team of seven, the same size as mine.

And choose only the brightest to come with you. Where? ... I'm sure you know where Dorado is, right? The old competition site on Axon.

"When you get here, we will chain Brad, Sophia, and Bridget together, and lock the amulet in a box which will be attached to all their chains. They will wait at the end of the final test, so the team that completes the challenges first will win the amulet.

"And you had better not even consider trying anything funny. Remember, we have the amulet, and your daughter. Plus, you've seen what our fleet is capable of.

"You have four hours to get here, not a minute longer."

Peter then made a signal for Quill to cut the transmission.

As Quill put the camera down, everyone looked at Peter like he wasn't the same person they had known for so long. They were used to Peter being a nervous, unsure, do-anything-to-avoid-confrontation type. But the speech he had just given was uncharacteristically aggressive.

"Glad I'm your friend," Neil remarked to Peter. "I certainly wouldn't want to get on your bad side."

"No kidding," Valerie said next. "Look at my arms. I was so moved that I got goosebumps."

CHAPTER 26

Not a single minute was wasted in the time leading up to Xavier's arrival (which could happen anytime in the next few hours.)

The first thing they did was go in to take a look at what was just inside the cave entrance.

"Check this out, Pete," Neil said, leading their group into the poorly lit area. "There are two big doors in here, and each one has a *wristband thingamajig* hanging on its doorknob."

"And look over here," Nicola said once her eyes had adjusted. "The instructions are posted on the wall between the two doors."

Peter walked over and stood beside Nicola to see what was written.

Rules

1. No more than 8 members per team.

2. A leader for each team must be

selected. He or she is to put on the wristband, which is hanging on the doorknob.

3. The two doors, which will take the two groups to their first challenge, must be opened simultaneously by the team leaders.

4. Each time a team completes a challenge, a green circle will light up on the opponent's wristband.

5. Any failed challenge results in disqualification, therefore automatic loss, of the entire competition.

Zoltan was kneeling down to look more closely at one of the wristbands (without touching it.)

"Thankfully these are nothing like the poison-filled one I had to wear before," he explained. "They are simply for the use outlined in the rules."

The only other thing of interest in here was the entrance to a narrow tunnel, labeled with a sign reading *"Judges and Award-bearers"*—indicating this path led directly to the end of the final challenge. (Spectators had no way of watching the competition while it was in progress, but at least they could wait at the end to congratulate the winners.)

"We might as well head back outside then," Peter told everyone, sounding a little disappointed. "Nothing here we can use to give us an advantage."

* * *

Although Valerie had only known Peter for a very short time, she could see how worried and stressed he was.

"Don't bottle your feelings up," she told him, putting her arm around his waist and leading him to a rock they could both sit down on. "Tell me exactly what's worrying you."

"Thanks, Val," Peter said after taking a seat. "But maybe it's best if I announce this concern to everyone."

"You're the boss," she smiled, lightly pinching his cheek. Then she raised her voice to call over the rest of the team. "Guys, Pete wants to tell everyone something! Can you all come over here for a sec?"

* * *

Peter's speech was just a *rehashing of things* he had told them before, but they still gave him their attention. He wanted to make absolutely sure that no one "waited" or "paused" on an idea while taking on these challenges.

"I am no more qualified or talented than any of you," he told them. "The second you get an idea— I don't care how absurd it is—just blurt it out, okay?"

He also needed (for the fifth time) to reconfirm

that when the challenges were done, they all remembered not to exit the mountain until after Zoltan gave them the word. (If they left the mountain while Xavier and his team were still on the surface, they'd be opening themselves up to an attack. They had to stay inside where weather god powers were nullified.)

* * *

"Just as I figured," Zoltan said, pointing to the sky at Xavier's approaching ship. "He must have flown here as fast as he could. It was less than thirty minutes ago when we told him he had four hours."

"Poker faces, guys," Peter told his team. "Let's do this."

CHAPTER 27

Peter and his team elected to wait just outside the cave entrance, so that they would be able to run inside if Xavier tried any trickery.

They had also retaped Jakayla's mouth and made sure her hands were tied firmly together behind her back. Zoltan was holding on to her wrists, making it appear she was being held against her will.

* * *

After Xavier's vessel landed and opened its ramp, Peter saw his brother and sister emerge, flanked by two very large men. Xavier had also decided to tape Bradley and Sophia's mouths shut (and bind their hands), likely as a way to spite Peter. (And it worked...)

"You guys okay?" Peter asked loudly.

They both nodded. At least they hadn't been hurt.

A few steps behind them, Xavier (in his gaudy golden cloak) strolled out with three middle-aged people on his left, and two somewhat older-looking fellows on his right.

"As you can see," Zoltan yelled to his brother. "Our team consists of seven. You'll have to leave one of yours behind."

"Don't try to boss me around, you imbecile," Xavier barked back. "My intel informed me that each team is permitted to have up to eight. You have only yourself to blame for showing up with an insufficient number."

"Zoltan," Peter said softly to him. "Don't sweat it. It shouldn't make much of a difference."

"Fine," Zoltan then said. "I guess that just goes to reinforce the fact that you could never beat me on even terms."

"Silence!" Xavier bellowed, raising his arms (to send a blast of wind.)

Peter and his friends—just like they had rehearsed—darted inside the cave (while Zoltan held the Bridget impersonator directly in front of himself.) If Xavier were to attack, he'd end up hitting *his daughter...*

"You sure play dirty," Xavier said, lowering his arms. "Tell those kids they can come back out. I won't harm anyone."

"Not a chance," Zoltan replied. "We shall continue this conversation inside the caves."

While making constant eye contact with his brother, he walked backward, pulling Jakayla along with him.

* * *

When Xavier's team was also inside, Zoltan showed them the lockable box that would be used to secure the amulet to Bradley, Sophia, and Bridget.

"I'm using this chain to connect all their wrists together," Zoltan explained while attaching it firmly to all three. "And I'm hanging the box with the amulet in it on Bridget's neck. The box itself, as you can see, is also attached to the chain.

"Prove the amulet is inside," Xavier demanded.

"Here's one of the two keys to the box," Zoltan said, throwing it to him. "Take a look for yourself."

Xavier slid the key in and twisted it. (Zoltan, meanwhile, made sure both of his hands were within centimeters of Jakayla's neck. This would ensure no unexpected movements by Xavier.)

"Beautiful," Xavier commented after looking in at the big amulet. Then he closed the box so it would relock. "Now stop acting like you think we are up to something here, you pathetic fool."

"The instructions are up on the wall over there," Peter then announced. "We'll give your team some time to—"

"I know what the rules are, Earthling boy," Xavier replied, mocking Peter. "My contacts stretch the galaxy far and wide." Then he started chuckling. "And when I depart this planet with the new amulet in my hands, my influence over the universe will soar exponentially."

CHAPTER 28

Just as Peter had expected, Xavier appointed himself the leader of the other team. The evil weather god put the band on his wrist while joking about its silliness. "If I wasn't required to wear this dumb thing in order to participate," he snarled. "Then I definitely wouldn't. I mean, think about it, what are the chances that these Earth bozos will solve any puzzles before us?"

Xavier's team let out a boisterous roar of laughter, all in agreement that their great leader had an intellect second to none.

Peter and Zoltan had a brief discussion about who would wear their team's bracelet. Zoltan felt Peter, who was indeed their true leader, should be the chosen one. But Peter pointed out a fact that couldn't be overlooked: he argued that Zoltan should wear it, just in case something came up later which would pit *leader against leader* at the end. Peter assumed that Zoltan knew more about Xavier's weak points than he did.

But after firmly reminding Peter that Xavier's powers were useless down here, and repeating his strong belief that Peter was by far the superior puzzler, Peter relented and put the band on his left wrist, just above his watch.

It was going to be "Team Xavier" against "Team Peter" today...

* * *

Since this site had been designed to allow a small group to be able to wait at the end of the final challenge (where they could award the victors their prize), Bradley, Sophia, and Jakayla (all chained together) got ready to walk down the narrow tunnel that would take them to that exact spot.

"Guys," Peter instructed those three. "DO NOT start walking through until both teams have entered their respective rooms and closed the doors behind them."

"Still don't trust me, do you?" Xavier commented, shaking his head.

Zoltan glared angrily at his older brother. (Xavier was, of course, much more powerful when it came to altering weather, but Zoltan figured he could probably take him down in hand-to-hand combat.) Zoltan's face hardened...

"Don't let him provoke you," Frederick told Zoltan calmly. "He's trying to rile you up because he knows it will throw your concentration off. Just ignore him."

"Thank you, Freddy," Zoltan smiled, taking a few deep breaths to calm himself down.

"Hurry up and put your hand on that stupid doorknob, boy," Xavier yelled to Peter, impatient to get started. "I don't have all day."

"Everyone ready?" Peter asked his team, (completely ignoring Xavier's comment.) "Any questions before we go in?"

"Dude," Neil said, walking up to give Peter a high-five. "Let's go kill these puzzles! I can't wait to watch Xavier and his cronies walk out with their tails between their legs."

Peter couldn't help but laugh a bit. "Well said, my man," he told his friend.

On the count of three, Xavier and Peter twisted their doorknobs clockwise, and both teams entered their rooms to begin this puzzling showdown.

CHAPTER 29

The room Peter and his team walked into seemed similar (in size) to a typical racquetball court, and had walls that rose at least five meters high.

The dimensions were *boring* compared to what it contained, though... (It almost seemed like they had been teleported to a 100-year-old watchmaker's shop.)

All the walls had numerous large clocks (mounted in a disorganized fashion.) There were at least fifteen or twenty on each wall. None of them were the modern, digital type, though; Every single clock had some type of pendulum hanging down, swinging back and forth. There were also at least ten free-standing grandfather clocks on the floor. All were beautiful antiques, just like the one Peter saw every summer in his grandparents' living room.

Within seconds of hearing the door close behind them, one of the clocks began chiming.

Bong, bong, bong, bong, bong, bong

Their eyes scoured the walls, looking to see which clock had just reached 6:00.

"It's that one, up there," Claire said, pointing at a rustic-colored one, high up near the ceiling on the left wall.

"Nice eye," Neil commended her.

"Um… Pete," Frederick then said, apparently having *beaten Peter to the punch* when it came to noticing something of significance. "These clocks are not only all set to different times, but the big hand is always somewhere between *:30* and *:59."*

Bong, bong

"There goes another one," Zoltan mentioned, pointing at the grandfather clock to his right that had just chimed 2:00.

Since their entire team had been looking around, no one initially paid any attention to the most mundane spot of this room: the inside of the spring-loaded door that had closed behind them after walking in.

"Guys!" Valerie called to everyone. "The instructions are posted on the door, right here! I'll read them for everyone."

"Read loudly," Frederick told his sister. "So we'll still be able to hear you when the next *inopportune* chimes start."

We all love clocks, now don't we?

Especially lovely antiques like these!

The beautiful chiming noise they emit on the hour is unmatched by the pathetic beeps made by today's silly digital ones...

Or perhaps you disagree? You like the new-age ones? Are we divided in opinion?

Anyway, enough of my ranting... Remember, you are not the only team trying to solve this!

Time limit: Thirty minutes

Number of attempts: 1

"It would appear even ancient Axons were sarcastic by nature," Zoltan commented after hearing the clue. "I bet Xavier threw a fit after reading it. He hates anything that could be interpreted as a mockery of his intelligence."

There was no confusion as to what they would be *attempting*. On the wall opposite the one they had entered, there were four doors, labeled with a large *1, 2, 3,* and *4.*

"Nik," Peter said to Nicola. "No pressure, but… well, you know that play-on-word puzzles like this one are right down your alley."

"I'll give it a shot," she answered. "Let me think it through a few times. Meanwhile, everyone should brainstorm their own ideas."

…

"Call me a simpleton," Neil then remarked. "But did any of you notice that the digit *1* is written right into the clue, almost like it's staring right at us?"

Number of attempts: 1

"In the previous line," he went on. "Where it says *'thirty minutes,'* the *thirty* is written as a word, not a digit. So maybe that means that the digit *1* is a hint, eh? Plus, if you omit *'of attempts'* from the last line, look what you are left with."

Number: 1

"Noted," Frederick said to Neil, doing a very Peteresque thing of jotting this down in a small notebook. "But let's explore other possibilities before trying anything."

* * *

Valerie, a big fan of mathematics and numbers, was contemplating if the use of the word *'divided'* in the clue came into play.

Are we divided in opinion?

"Pete," she said, now standing very close to him. (Close enough to make Nicola wonder if Valerie lacked the understanding of personal space!) "Convince me the word *divided* is irrelevant."

"Divided, eh?" Peter pondered. "Division... Divisible by... Hmm..." He paused after thinking about it a little more. "I can't say it is *definitely meaningless.* Run with it, Val."

"Gotcha," she smiled, lightly putting her hand on his left triceps. Then she leaned in close and whispered. "There is one thing I'm not *divided* about, but I'll tell you about that later." Then she winked and took a few steps back.

Nicola had unintentionally seen that little exchange, and she immediately felt anger (or possibly jealousy?) well up inside. She had managed to *fight off* Claire before, but was she now up against Valerie?

* * *

"There are ninety clocks in total," Zoltan announced a bit later. "I'm not saying that that number means anything, but it could come in handy, I suppose."

"Ninety clocks, eh?" Valerie pondered. "And in

the note, we have the word '*thirty,*' where it says '*thirty minutes.*' Ninety… and thirty… Ninety divided by thirty… Freddy, come here! Add this to your list!"

$$90 \div 30 = 3$$

"I like your theory better than mine," Neil mentioned.

The chiming wasn't constant, but it was occurring regularly. (Two or three clocks went off every minute, chiming anywhere from one to twelve times.) So yes, this was a pretty noisy and distracting atmosphere to think in…

* * *

"Here's something we haven't considered yet," Claire suddenly said when they were closing in on fifteen minutes since stating. "No one has looked to see *how many* of the clocks will chime to 1:00, 2:00, 3:00, and 4:00. What do you think?"

"I'll help you count," Neil then said to her. "I'll count the ones and twos. You do the threes and fours."

* * *

"There are zero clocks near 1:00," Neil said a minute later. "And four near 2:00."

"I've got two near 3:00, and thirteen near 4:00," Claire said next.

Valerie had come over while listening to those numbers. "Say those again, guys," she told them, now holding Frederick's notebook. "I want to write this down."

Then she did some math...

$$For\ 1{:}00 \qquad 0 \div 1 = 0$$
$$For\ 2{:}00 \qquad 4 \div 2 = 2$$
$$For\ 3{:}00 \qquad 2 \div 3 = 0.67$$
$$For\ 4{:}00 \qquad 13 \div 4 = 3.15$$

"Pete, check this out!" Valerie said with some spunk. "Only one of these four equations produces a whole number."

"Ah..." Peer smiled, looking at her notes.

$$For\ 2{:}00 \qquad 4 \div 2 = 2$$

"Well, it would now seem we have reasons to choose doors 1, 2, and 3..." Zoltan commented.

...

Peter heard some type of beeping noise, although he wasn't sure where it was coming from.

"Your wristband is flashing, dude," Neil pointed out.

Peter looked down and saw a green circle now glowing.

"Oh man, Xavier's team is already finished this one," Peter told everyone. "C'mon, we gotta hurry!"

This news, coupled with the fact they only had seven minutes to go, caused the bulk of Peter's team to start panicking to various degrees.

The coolest one of the bunch was Nicola, who was still busy pondering if something was hiding within the words in the instructions...

Bong, bong, bong, bong, bong

Nicola looked around to see which clock had just chimed, but she couldn't find any showing 5:00.

"That one over there just got to 4:00," Neil pointed out. "You sure it didn't chime four times?"

"It was five, I'm positive," she told Neil. Then she got thinking again... "Neil, quickly help me find which one will hit 4:00 or 5:00 next."

* * *

Less than a minute later, one of the wall clocks—mounted low on the right side—chimed five times after reaching 5:00.

...

Nicola reread the clue and thought more deeply about what had just happened. "Hmm..." she wondered quietly.

...

"Guys!" she yelled. "Everyone watch this grandfather clock here for a second. Actually, *listen to it* is what I meant to say..."

All eyes were on the clock she was pointing to, which was about to reach 4:00.

Bong, bong, bong, bong, bong

...

"It's door 4 that we want!" Nicola then cheered after it chimed.

"Are you sure?" Valerie said, confused. "I mean, I'll admit that it is intriguing that this big clock here just hit 4:00 but chimed *five* times. But, uh... that could just be a technical malfunction. I—"

"No, I'm sure I'm right!" said Nicola, shutting down Valerie's doubts. "The same thing happened with another clock that hit 4:00. That can't be a coincidence. And get this, the clue says '*chiming noise they emit on the hour is unmatched...*' *Unmatched!* Those clocks are showing 4:00, but chiming FIVE times. So they don't match! *Unmatched,* right?"

"Open it, Pete," Neil told his friend while high-fiving Nicola. "You're the one wearing the wristband."

Peter looked at Nicola (who seemed very confident) and then at Valerie (who looked very hesitant...)

116

"We still have a few more minutes to think things through," Valerie said to Peter. "If we act before we are 100% sure, and end up being wrong, we lose…"

…

"I'm going with my intuition here," Peter answered, putting his hand on the *4-doorknob.* "Nik said she's sure about this, and I see no reason to doubt her."

…

It opened!

"Yahoo!" Neil cheered. "Now hurry up, we have some catching up to do."

Beep, beep

"Bad news, guys," Peter said while running through the door. "A second green circle just came on… Xavier's team has already finished the second puzzle, too!"

CHAPTER 30

Neil, the last one through the door, quickly closed it. (He wanted to see if the instructions for challenge two were also posted on its inside.)

Nope...

The area they had just entered was fairly dark. There was only one light bulb—which likely had a reasonable amount of dust on it—thus preventing it from working well.

"No rules here, guys," Neil told the team, spinning around to look at their next puzzle. "Yikes, this is... like, WAY different from anything I ever would have guessed..."

"No kidding," Nicola agreed. "It almost doesn't look like a puzzle at all."

They were standing at the start of a long, narrow hallway, probably close to ten meters in total length. The one and only thing of interest here, which began just in front of them and continued almost to the other end, was... well, something they would never have expected to see underground.

"Guys," Neil then said to everyone. "This is totally like the things they have at the international terminal of Stoneburg Airport. You know, it's like an escalator, except it doesn't go up or down; It's flat."

"Plus," Claire added. "This one here is actually a conveyor belt instead of *moving steps,* kind of like on treadmills at the gym."

There was no space between the side handrails and the walls: meaning the only way to get to the exit was by using the conveyor belt.

But there was a big difference between the ones used to assist tired passengers at the airport and the one in front of them now: this one was spinning (rapidly) the wrong way! It wouldn't take someone to the other end; It would just push whoever tried to use it back to the start!

Yikes...

"Step aside, my friends," Neil remarked while stretching his legs. "I used to run up the down escalator, or down the up, all the time at the mall when I was a kid. But man, did it ever make my mom mad..."

"That would have been quite unsafe," Frederick pointed out. "Why would someone do a silly thing like that?"

"Neil's thought process is not the same as that of a normal person," Peter laughed. "He does stuff that's weird because, well, HE is weird, simple as that."

Neil jumped onto the backward-spinning belt and awkwardly tried running. He was giving it a good go, but barely making any forward process.

About twenty seconds after starting this mad dash, but not even one-third of the way across, he gave up and let it bring him back to the start.

"Before anyone else tests their athleticism," Zoltan commented. "Perhaps we should examine our surroundings a little more. There might be a way to slow it down, or even stop the spinning."

* * *

They performed a quick (but thorough) scan of the walls and floor near the entrance, pushing on each and every brick in the hopes of finding a secret button.

* * *

"Val," Neil said to her, realizing there was one place they hadn't checked yet. "Get on my shoulders. I'll boost you up so you can reach the bricks on the ceiling."

* * *

Nothing of consequence up there...

"Hey," Claire then thought aloud. "Think the entrance door itself might function as a button?

Maybe opening it will stop, or reverse, the spinning of the belt."

"Definitely worth a shot," Peter agreed.

The door they had previously come through was not lockable, so she easily reopened it. But unfortunately, that didn't affect the spinning speed or direction...

"Claire, you're pretty fast, eh?" Neil said to his ex. "Since this door is open now, you could go back into the first room and take a big run-up. If you get enough momentum going, you might be able to make it across."

"And maybe a button to shut this thing off is at the opposite end?" Claire mentioned. "It's possible that only one of us has to sprint down that belt."

Claire took off her backpack and handed it to Neil. "Watch and learn," she smiled. "I'll show you the definition of *lightning fast.*"

To give her as much space as possible, everyone else went back into the first room and stood at the sides. They also shifted a couple of the big grandfather clocks out of the way to give her a clear path through.

...

"Go, girl! Go!" Neil said, encouraging Claire.

Claire bolted toward the conveyor belt. She was moving quite fast when she got there, but her first step on the belt caused her to lose her footing. She was able to recover, but most of her momentum was gone.

...

She was now going all out, and had just passed the halfway mark.

...

"You're almost there!" Nicola yelled. "Keep going!"

...

But about fifteen seconds later, it was easy to see she had stopped making forward progress. When she realized this for herself, she stopped running, and turned around.

...

"Drat," she told everyone as the belt quickly sent her back to the start. "If I hadn't tripped over my own feet, I might have been able to get there."

"Let me give it another go," Neil said next. "I've got the longest legs here. I should be able to *Usain Bolt* my way across."

...

Neil made it a little past halfway this time, but then he ran out of steam.

...

"Before anyone else tries," Zoltan said, thinking they were missing something here. "Let me point this out: No one on Xavier's team is even close to as fast as Neil or Claire. I can't imagine any of them being capable of outrunning the belt."

* * *

"Since we still don't have a new idea," Claire said a few minutes later (after she had caught her breath.) "I'm gonna take another shot at sprinting across."

...

This time, her jump from the floor to the conveyor went perfectly.

...

And she got halfway down easily.

...

Then (although looking drained) she reached the three-quarter spot.

As she tired, her progress slowed more and more. But she was not going to allow the burning in her legs to force her to give up again. She pressed on, harder and harder.

When she got about ninety percent of the way to the end, her failing legs told her it was time to shut down. In desperation, she dove.

She was close, a matter of centimeters in fact, but not close enough...

Angry at herself, she sat down on the conveyor, which started bringing her back.

Then she stood up and grabbed the handrails for balance. One arm moved along in sync with her body, but her other arm was ripped backward hard by the other handrail.

"Ouch!" she screamed in pain.

She didn't have enough time to stand up on her own again before getting back to the start, so Neil had to grab her when she got there.

"What just happened?" Neil asked her. "Leg cramp?"

Claire spun around to check the cause of her fall...

...

Then she noticed it!

"Now we know why this area is so poorly lit," she explained. "Look at the two handrails. This one, on our left, is moving in sync with the conveyor belt. But the right handrail is spinning in the opposite direction!"

Peter came up to check this out for himself. "You're right," he said.

Neil didn't need any instructions: He knew exactly what to do. (He was already sitting on the right handrail, legs dangling, being carried to the end.)

* * *

"There's no button over here," he yelled back after getting off the handrail in front of the exit. "You've all gotta do the same thing I just did."

A minute later, they had all joined Neil.

"That was pretty tricky," Frederick commented. "But I don't see what the *puzzle* was here…"

"Freddy," Zoltan said to him. "It was designed to force us to remove our preconceived view of what we were dealing with. No one would ever guess that a handrail next to a conveyor belt would be rigged up to spin the opposite way, would they?"

"Of course not," Frederick replied. "That would be pointless…" Then Frederick smiled. "This is a little off-topic, but hey, this conveyor belt trick just gave me a new puzzle idea for my next book."

"Pete," Valerie said, taking one hand as he opened the door with the other. "This is turning out to be kind of fun, isn't it?"

CHAPTER 31

"Peter," Zoltan asked, wanting to confirm something. "Is your wristband still showing two circles?"

"Yup," he replied. "But Xavier's been working on the third puzzle for a while already. They've got a pretty big head start on us."

"But we've got you, Pete," Valerie (who was still holding Peter's hand) said, winking again. "I like our odds."

At that moment, Frederick seemed to pick up on the fact that his elder sister *"had the hots"* for his new friend. (He refrained from actually making a comment, but his facial expression said it all...)

Nicola, also unimpressed by the hand holding, started to wonder if Peter's real reason for bringing Valerie along was for something other than her ability to solve puzzles.

...

The square chamber they were now standing in, which was not much bigger than Peter's living room, immediately took Peter, Neil, and Nicola's minds back to one of the puzzles they had tackled against Xavier many, many years ago.

"The floor here is just like the *checkerboard one* we did way back in Grade 7," Nicola said to Peter while boldly taking his other hand.

"Totally," Neil added. "Except these tiles have arrows on them, instead of numbers."

Other than a strip of stone inside the door they had just walked through, which was maybe a meter wide, the entire floor was just like a big checkerboard. Each square was about 60-by-60 centimeters in size. (And the "board" was 8 tiles wide and 8 tiles long.)

Each tile had a large, yellow arrow on it, and all of these arrows pointed in one of four directions: straight ahead, to the left, to the right, or backward.

At first glance, there didn't appear to be any specific order or system to the arrow placement. It seemed more or less random.

...

"Look up," Frederick told everyone. "Our clue happens to be on the ceiling this time. "

They all craned their necks to check out what

had been carved into the stone ceiling.

"Suppose that's our way across," Zoltan commented.

Unlike the room with the *numbered checkerboard* they did in the past, this one looked like it involved more than simply making it across, though.

There were five archways (all unlabeled), only one of which was likely the correct way out. Three of those five were on the far wall (one in the center, one close to the right side, and one close to the left side.) And the other two archways were actually on the side walls, both in the location of the third-last row of tiles.

Peter and Frederick (without consulting each other) had both already removed pencils and notebooks from their backpacks. (They certainly did think alike!) They copied down the clue so they wouldn't have to keep twisting their heads up to see it.

"Pete," Frederick then suggested. "Why don't we split up and brainstorm separately? That might lead to a few more ideas."

"Good thinking," Peter agreed. "I'll work with Claire, Nik, and Neil over here. You team up with your sister and Zoltan. And you guys stand over there, so we can't overhear each other."

* * *

Although they were technically *"one team of 7,"* Peter really wanted to crack this puzzle before Frederick's group. His silly pride didn't want to admit that he might not be the most capable puzzler here today…

(Peter, forget your stupid pride! There are bigger things at stake here!)

"Okay, guys," Frederick said softly to his sister and Zoltan. "There are four sets of arrows in the clue, right? Well, technically there are three sets of two arrows, and the final one is a single arrow only."

↑→   ↓←   →↑   ↑

"My first instinct," Valerie commented. "Based mostly on the fact that people have two feet, is that the clue is telling us which arrow sets we have to put our feet in while moving across."

"Cool," Frederick grinned. "Then we are on the same page."

A quick scan of the area near the start of the checkerboard showed them they had three places where they could start with one foot in a ↑ and one in a →.

"So how do we pick?" Zoltan asked the brother-sister duo.

"It will depend on which one of those three sets is close enough to jump to the next set indicated in the clue, a backward arrow and a left arrow," Frederick answered.

"Sorry, but I've got two more questions," Zoltan said back. "One, do we have to get across in only four leaps? And two, for the fourth set, which is only a single forward-facing arrow, do we have to land both feet in the same square? Or each foot in separate forward-arrow squares?"

"Hmm…" Frederick pondered, jotting these unknowns down.

* * *

Peter's team had been working on the same theory. And they had also settled on the assumption that the trip across was required to be done in only four jumps.

"Okay, I'll show you the path I think looks doable," Nicola said while pointing at the squares. "First those two, then those two there. Third, those two. And lastly, that one."

"Then you're saying for the last one, both feet go in one square?" Peter asked, wanting confirmation.

"That seems to make the most sense to me," she replied.

"That means your path would put us in front of the archway on the left wall," Claire mentioned.

"Freddy!" Peter called to the other group. "We've got a way across we are thinking of trying.

How about you guys?"

"Yeah, us too," he replied. "Which door does yours lead to?"

"The one on the left wall," Peter told him. "You?"

"Middle door on the far wall," Frederick answered.

Hmm...

After quickly comparing notes, they realized the two teams had mapped out completely different paths.

"So how do we decide which one to try?" Claire asked. "There can't be two solutions."

As much as Peter wanted to be right, he had to admit that Frederick's path across was more appealing, for two reasons. First, Nicola's path involved making one "quite awkward" jump. And second, getting to the opposite wall (as opposed to one of the side walls) just seemed a little more sensible.

"Let's try yours," Peter told Freddy. "Neil, you up for this?"

"You bet, dude," Neil replied. "I just hope these tiles don't drop away into an abyss like the checkerboard we did a few years back."

(Gulp! Peter had kind of forgotten about that...)

Neil jumped to the first set (a ↑ and a →) that

Frederick was pointing to. His left foot landed on the → at the same time as his right foot landed on the ↑.

Both squares depressed about two centimeters into the ground, making him feel like he was stepping on the buttons of a gigantic calculator.

And both tiles were now glowing green.

"Cool," Neil remarked, looking at the bright tiles beneath his feet. "I supposed green is good, isn't it?"

After double-checking with Frederick about where his next leap was headed, Neil got ready to jump.

"Standing broad jump, just like in elementary school," he joked.

The instant his feet left the ground, the two squares returned to their original positions, and the glowing stopped.

Neil easily landed on the ↓ and the ← he was headed for. The tile under his left foot glowed green, but the one under his right foot was red!

"Not good," Neil commented, freezing in place. "Umm... a little help here, guys?"

Everyone was expecting *something* to happen, likely something bad...

...

"You seem to be taking your sweet time," Neil said while starting to panic. "C'mon, bail me out here."

Frederick and Peter briefly chatted, and concluded that the safest option was for Neil to retrace his steps back to the start. But this, of course, meant he would have to jump backward. They thought spinning around would be too risky, because that would require briefly lifting each foot, meaning no pressure would be applied to the squares for a fraction of a second, (and they weren't sure if that was okay or not.)

"You can do this!" Claire yelled. "Take your time, babe. You've got this."

Neil thankfully pulled off this *reverse leap,* landing both feet in the squares he had previously been in. But the instant his foot left the red square, a laser beam started shooting out of it up to the ceiling!

"Dudes," Neil said, looking at the beam. "I can feel the laser's heat from here. It would melt human flesh like butter."

"Let's hope it shuts off soon," Zoltan mentioned.

Neil then made his second backward jump, landing on the strip of stone near the entrance.

But the laser beam remained constant...

you're not expecting me to be your

guinea pig for the next attempt across?" Neil asked while sitting cross-legged on the floor.

"Unfortunately," Peter said, patting Neil's shoulder. "You've got the longest legs. You are better suited for big jumps than any of us."

"Kind of thought you'd say that," Neil sighed. "Anyway, just give me a minute."

* * *

This time, Neil was going to attempt the route that would take him to the opening on the left wall: the one suggested by Nicola.

...

He thankfully got green lights on his first and second leaps, but when he landed on the third set, a → and a ↑, both glowed red!

"Okay, this officially sucks," Neil mumbled.

...

"Don't move!" Nicola suddenly yelled. "I think I have an idea!"

Nicola's theory was somewhere between *brilliant* and *crazy.* Her thinking was as follows: knowing the laser beams wouldn't start shooting until the instant Neil's feet came off the two tiles he was applying pressure to, then why not have Neil stay exactly where he was?

(WHAT!?)

"The next person," Nicola went on, outlining her plan. "Let's say, Claire: jumps along the same path Neil just used. She then lands in the same squares Neil is currently in, which will be tricky but not impossible. After that, Neil could then jump out of those to the final forward-facing arrow tile. The lasers won't come on when Neil jumps to that tile because Claire will now be standing on those two red tiles. Then, finally, Neil goes out the archway on the left wall.

"If we were to proceed like this, then the laser beams wouldn't deploy until the seventh and final person on our team jumps out of those two squares. At that point, it wouldn't matter, because everyone else will already be past them."

* * *

"Intriguing," Frederick commented. "I like it. Pete, you?"

"Oh yeah," Peter smiled.

Claire volunteered to be the test subject for this idea.

...

As planned, she followed the path Neil had jumped along, and eventually landed in the same two squares Neil's feet were currently in. (Neil had *braced for impact,* as he didn't want to lose his balance and fall out if she bumped him too hard.)

After landing, Claire wrapped her arms around him from behind. (Not as a gesture of intimacy, but to prevent herself and him from falling.) "Just like old times, eh?" she joked in his left ear.

"You know where you are headed, right?" Freddy called to Neil. "Land both feet in the forward-facing arrow, the one directly in front of the archway on the side wall. And Claire, make sure you don't lift your feet while he's doing this."

...

But when Neil landed both feet in the ↑ he had been aiming for, it glowed red!

"But that technically doesn't matter," Nicola pointed out to everyone. "We can still all get out safely using the system I just suggested."

Nicola then prepared to get started as the third person of this *train.* (Neil and Claire, of course, stood still... They couldn't go anywhere until Nicola arrived.)

But just before Nicola started, Neil noticed something. "Guys!" he yelled. "A gate is lowering from the ceiling here! It's gonna block this archway! We can't use this one to get out!"

Uh oh...

Thirty seconds later, that exit had been closed off.

"The other four archways still look okay," Zoltan told everyone. "You need to carefully make your way back. But Claire, wait for Neil to land in your squares before you jump out. If you move early, he'll get fried by the lasers."

Neil's jump back was going to be tricky. (But at least he could turn around before jumping, since pivoting his feet while keeping pressure on the single square was easy.) The awkward part was that he would be landing in the two squares Claire was standing in, which were a fair distance away. Claire shuffled her feet as far back as she could, to provide Neil with a slightly bigger landing pad.

Neil's awkward leap couldn't have gone any worse. He jumped way too far, slamming hard into Claire's body.

There was no way for poor Claire to keep her balance. She fell backward, and now her lower back and shoulders were depressing two new tiles.

"You okay?" Neil yelled in fear, briefly contemplating an attempt to grab her as she fell. (But his sudden movement caused his center of gravity to get thrown off. He didn't want to fall on her, so he ended up toppling to his left, and now his left hip and shoulder were depressing two new tiles!)

Both of Claire's squares were green, so she could simply stand up.

But both of Neil's were red! (And one of those two was directly in front of the left-most archway on the far wall, and a gate was now closing in that one!)

After standing up in her two new squares, Claire then jumped (following Frederick's instructions) back to the start.

But Neil was kind of, umm, trapped…

The ↑ he had had both feet in near the left-wall archway was shooting a laser up, and so were the two tiles he had just shared with Claire… So, this board now had four hot lasers firing.

"Neil," Peter instructed him. "Don't move."

"You just want me to lie here?" Neil asked back.

"For now, yes," Peter answered. "Until we figure out how to get you back here."

(Now what!?)

CHAPTER 32

"Guys!?" Claire said once she was safely back at the start again. "We can't leave Neil out there... What are we gonna do!?"

* * *

Since four powerful lasers were now blasting up from the floor, the room was gradually heating up. The armpits of Peter's shirt (which would have been at least a little wet on a normal day), were drenched. It looked like he had just run a marathon.

Now they were really in a pinch... Two of the three viable paths they had mapped out were wrong. And the only way to get across using the third reachable ↑ and → set would involve making a "historic-sized leap" halfway through...

They were, for lack of a better term, stumped. (Plus, Neil was trapped!)

Neil had rolled onto his back to get a little more

comfortable. He needed to keep his hands and feet up in the air, to prevent them from accidentally pushing down on any more tiles. (He looked like a cockroach that had just been sprayed with bug killer!) Since he had nothing better to do now, he began looking at the clue carved in the ceiling near the entrance.

"Forward-right, back-left, right-forward, forward," he said robotically. "Forward-right, back-left, right-forward, forward. Forward-right-back-left-right-forward-forward…"

Then he did a little math. (Not his forte, but hey, anyone can do simple addition, right?)

"Three *forwards,* one *backward,* two *rights,* one *left,*" he mumbled.

…

"Guys!" Neil then yelled. "Listen to this!"

"What's up?" Peter asked back.

"Let's assume, just for a minute," Neil began. "That the clue is NOT telling us where we have to plant our feet while moving across the board."

"Um…" Peter commented, doubtful. "Okay??"

"So if we forget that," Neil went on. "Then here's what we've got: Three forward arrows, one backward arrow, two right arrows, and one left arrow."

"And...?" Peter asked while sketching this in his notebook.

"I think it might be telling us that the *'direction'* to head in," Neil went on. "First, we can cancel some out, right? A forward one cancels the backward arrow. And a right one cancels the left arrow"

"Hmmm..." Peter pondered.

"That leaves us with two forwards and a right," Peter then said.

"Back in boy scouts," Neil commented, "we would call that north-north-east."

Frederick quickly removed a compass from his backpack. "Get this everyone," he said right away. "The forward-facing arrows on the floor in here point perfectly north."

"Sweet!" Neil cheered.

"Hold on a second," Peter said to everyone. "But we wouldn't have had any way to know that if Freddy hadn't brought a compass."

"True," Frederick agreed. "But maybe this puzzle could be solved the same way by simply assuming that *forward equals north.*"

"So, if you stand at the start of the board," Neil

asked loudly. "Halfway between the two side walls—which is where we were right after walking in—then where would north-north-east point?"

"Directly at one of the archways on the far wall," Frederick answered. "The one closest to the right-side wall."

"That's what I was hopin' you'd say!" Neil cheered.

"But how do we get there?" Valerie asked.

"The path we use to get across shouldn't matter at all," Frederick pointed out to his sister. "Since we now know the arrows on the floor mean nothing."

"I suggest we also apply Nik's system for moving across safely," Claire added. "Why don't we use the second column of squares from the right wall, which will take us in a straight line to the door we are headed for. The first person jumps, with both feet together, into the first square of that column. The next person joins him in that square. Then the first person jumps out to row two. Then the third person joins the second person. Et cetera."

"Simplicity and teamwork at its best," Peter smiled.

"What about Neil?" Zoltan wondered.

"Well," Frederick suggested. "He should just stand up in one of the two squares he's currently occupying, making sure to maintain constant pressure on it. If he then moves along the squares on the far wall, jumping with both feet into one square each time, he'll be able to get to the exit no problem."

"But you guys go first!" Neil yelled. "If I get stuck behind, no big deal: you can fish me out later. But you guys HAVE TO complete this test."

* * *

It was fairly time-consuming, but all six (everyone minus Neil) were moving across without any surprises. The first four squares they had used were *red* ones, meaning four more lasers were now shooting up.

* * *

(And luckily, a gate did not drop down in this archway!)

* * *

Five of the "train of six people" were now in the tunnel just beyond the archway.

Only Peter (who was the last person of the train) and Neil (still lying on the ground) remained on the checkerboard.

"Up you come," Peter told his friend. "I'm not leaving you behind."

Neil switched all his weight to the square his shoulders were on, meaning a laser was now coming from the one his butt had just come off. He then stood up and two-foot jumped to the next square along the wall. Of course, that meant another laser shot up, right behind him. (But they were both expecting that.)

Neil then jumped square by square, finally landing in Peter's square.

"Told you you'd be fine," Peter smiled. "Please don't tell me you were so terrified back there that you peed your pants?"

"Very funny," Neil laughed, playfully pushing Peter into the tunnel.

Neil then followed him in.

They had done it! Not only that, but Xavier's team hadn't finished yet!

Team Peter was in the lead!

CHAPTER 33

"Neil, you were awesome back there!" Claire said once the whole team had walked through the short tunnel to the chamber containing their next challenge. She gave him a big hug, followed by a peck on the cheek.

Peter hadn't noticed the hug and kiss—not that he would have cared anyway—as he was completely focusing on the newest challenge.

"Those two would make a cute couple," Valerie said to Peter while watching Neil and Claire.

Peter didn't feel like launching into the history of Neil and Claire's relationship, so he just smiled and said, "Yeah, probably."

Then Valerie took Peter's hand (again) and leaned in close to his ear. "And they're not the only two here that I see as a perfect match, if you know what I mean," she whispered. And she followed that with a peck on Peter's left cheek!

Peter immediately looked around to see who had (or hadn't) witnessed that completely unexpected kiss. Everyone was ahead of him and Valerie by a few steps, and (other than Zoltan) they had all been looking forward.

Zoltan ever so slightly nodded and smiled, as if communicating to Peter that he approved of this new pairing.

"What have we here?" Frederick said, now standing in the center of this round, stone room, which was about three meters across. "There's a pedestal with a red button on top, but I don't see any rules or instructions anywhere."

"Don't press it yet," Zoltan said right away. "Let's inspect things first."

Frederick giggled a little. "Of course, I wasn't planning on pushing it until we were ready," he commented, rolling his eyes in jest. "I'm not stupid."

"Academically, you're a genius," his sister mentioned. "But if we are talking about common sense, you certainly aren't the sharpest knife in the drawer."

Everyone, including Frederick, laughed at that comment.

This room, similar to the challenge they had just completed, also had several archways to exit from. This time there were six in total, equally spaced around the circular room.

Above all six exits, there were thin signs (made

of stone and about 30-by-30 centimeters in size.) But what was on those signs was baffling... each one had only a single word on it.

Starting next to the door they had just used to enter, and going clockwise, the six exit tunnel signs read: *I, My, You, Your, He,* and *His.*

"Reminds me of Mr. Forrester's Grade 1 class," Neil joked. Then he tried to mimic his former teacher's deep voice. "Now don't mess up your pronouns, kids."

"Kind of makes me think of conjugating verbs in French class," Peter said next, laughing a bit. ... But his *playful demeanor* quickly changed when his wristband started beeping. "Bad news; Xavier has just caught up."

They didn't need much time to realize this challenge came without a hint, seeing as there was nothing written on the ceiling, walls, or floor.

"But for all we know," Nicola mentioned. "Maybe we receive a clue after pushing the button."

"Possibly," Zoltan added. "Or, well... the button could even start some kind of countdown."

"Since there are seven of us," Peter said, thinking aloud. "Here's an idea: one of us stands in front of each exit, and Freddy will be in charge of pushing the button."

"What should we be watching for?" Claire asked.

"Not sure," Peter replied honestly. "Just keep your eyes peeled."

* * *

"Pushing it now," Frederick announced when everyone was in place.

...

"Anything?" Peter asked a few seconds later.

"Up there!" Frederick yelled, pointing at a hole that had just opened up in the ceiling.

Peter (disobeying his own instructions) ran to Frederick's side so he could see it better.

A few seconds later, a blast of air could be felt coming from that hole. It wasn't cold or hot or smoky or anything like that; It was simply just a stream of wind.

And after about twenty seconds of that, the hole closed.

Frederick and Peter looked at each other and shrugged their shoulders.

"That was weird," Frederick went to say. (But the pitch of his voice was more than an octave higher than usual. He sounded like that famous mouse from the world's most popular theme park!)

"What are you—?" Peter started to comment, his voice also really high now.

The two started laughing, and the rest of the team took that as a sign that they could leave their posts at the other exits.

"Stop fooling around," Neil joked (in an unbelievably high voice!)

The 10-year-old inside each of the teenagers spent the next thirty seconds saying all sorts of pointless comments, laughing away at how ridiculous they sounded.

...

Soon, their voices returned to normal.

Valerie, however, looked a little concerned.

"You okay?" Frederick asked her. "You feel faint or something?"

"No, I'm fine," she told him. "I'm just worried that we might have squandered our chance there. Maybe we were supposed to read what's written on those six signs while our voices were high-pitched. That might have been the way to determine which exit is right."

"Ahh..." Neil pondered. "You mean like when a singer breaks a glass with her voice?"

Hmm...

"Freddy, you're gonna push it again," Peter then instructed him. "But this time, we all stay in front of our exits, completely silent. Freddy will yell the six words on the signs when his voice is high-pitched again."

* * *

"I! My! You! Your! He! His!" Freddy screamed in a voice that was so unbelievably high that it was hard for his teammates to stifle their laughs.

The other six were looking both at the sign above their exit (to see if it cracked or something) and into the exit itself. They were waiting for "something" to indicate which archway was correct.

"Well?" Peter asked, voice high again. "Anyone?"

Silence...

* * *

"Dang!" Peter said, hearing a different noise: one coming from his wristband. "Xavier's team just solved another one."

...

They needed to try a different approach, and Nicola was the one to suggest something. "Let's count the number of each letter in these six signs," she recommended.

I: 2
M: 1
Y: 3
O: 2

U: 2
R: 1
H: 2
E: 1
S: 1

Hmm...

"Well, there are more *Y's* than any other letter," Nicola said to Peter.

"But three of the six signs have a *Y* in them," Peter mentioned.

"True," she admitted. "But only the *Y* in 'My' sounds like a *Y.* It's used as a consonant in the other two: You don't hear the Y-vowel-sound in 'You' or 'Your.'"

"Sorry to be a Negative Nelly," Zoltan told her, wanting to be honest. "But that seems a little far-fetched to me."

"I know," Nicola smiled, not offended in the least. "Let me keep working on it; I'll tell you if I come up with something."

* * *

"Pete," Valerie said, following Peter as he paced around the room. "Can I talk to you when we have finished all these puzzles today?"

Peter stopped walking, and looked her right into the eyes. (Her beautiful, mesmerizing *peepers* briefly took his attention away from where it needed to be...) "Sure," he replied. "What about?"

"I think you know," she answered, planting another kiss on his cheek (which hopefully no one spotted.) "Now hurry up and crack this puzzle, champ."

One interesting thing that Zoltan had noticed was how Peter and Frederick's tendencies were very similar. Frederick was also pacing around, mumbling away to himself indecipherably.

Zoltan pointed this out to Neil, who found it not only interesting but also very entertaining. Neil then stood up and started blatantly imitating the two "pacing thinkers."

Claire giggled when she noticed Neil's antics, but this immature behavior rubbed Nicola the wrong way.

"Stop that," she scolded Neil. "You're acting like a buffoon."

Neil realized he was wasting energy and distracting his teammates, so he softly said, "Sorry," and sat back down.

Frederick, who had been so immersed in his thoughts that he had only heard the last word that Nicola had said, asked, "What balloon?"

Peter started laughing. "Not balloon," he told Frederick. *"Buffoon.* She just called Neil a buffoon, which we all, of course, know he is."

That comment, thankfully, lightened the mood a little.

...

Frederick then got an expression on his face: which could only mean one thing... He had figured it out!!

He ran over to high-five Neil. "Nice work, you big buffoon!" he joked. Then he spun around to explain the solution to his eagerly waiting audience. "Guys, you've all been to birthday parties, right? And birthday parties, as you know, usually have balloons."

"And buffoons, if I'm invited," Neil said while laughing.

"The word *balloon* reminded me of my friend Jeremy's tenth birthday bash," Frederick explained. "His mom invited every kid on the block, and she went all out for that party. There was a bouncy castle, a magician, a hot dog stand, a cotton candy machine, and balloons... TONS of balloons!"

...

"I may seem like a super serious person now," Frederick went on. "But back then, I was known to be a little silly on occasion. Anyway, when we realized that those balloons were the type that floated, Jeremy challenged each kid to open one up, breathe in some of its contents, and then try talking in a *funny high voice.*"

"Just like what happened here…" Zoltan nodded. "What gas do they use to make balloons float? You know, on Earth?"

"Helium," Peter answered.

…

"Yes, indeed… Helium," Frederick smiled. "And the chemical symbol for Helium is *He… He!* And that door has a big *'He'* above it!"

"Superb analytical skills!" Zoltan applauded him. "Now c'mon, Xavier is almost neck and neck with us! We don't want to lose our lead again!"

CHAPTER 34

The dark tunnel they entered gradually curved to the right. After shuffling along for seven or eight meters, they saw a door at its end. There was a small light in the ceiling, pointing directly at a sign on that door.

Only 4 continue

"Not surprised," Zoltan sighed. "Actually, I thought they would have forced us to whittle down our numbers a little earlier."

"Well, this one's a no-brainer," Neil said. "Pete, Zoltan, Nik, and Freddy. Our *all-stars!*"

"Thank you for sharing your thoughts," Zoltan said to Neil. "But we will defer this decision to Peter." Then he turned to face their leader. "Sorry to rush you, but we are in a race; Every second counts."

"Don't you think Val should keep going instead of Nik?" Frederick suggested timidly. "As her sibling, I can tell you she ROCKS when it comes to solving puzzles. But then again, maybe I'm biased because we're related."

Valerie looked quite happy to be praised by her younger brother. "I'm up for it," she told everyone confidently.

Nicola didn't want Peter's thought process to be coerced or influenced by Valerie's constant flirting, so she stood right in between the two. Every time Valerie tried to step to one side or the other, Nicola shadowed her.

Peter hated pressure (of any sort), but he especially despised the type where he was forced to choose between friends.

...

"Guys," Peter said fifteen seconds later. "I hate *picking favorites,* but hey, I've got no other option here... I'm taking Zoltan, Freddy, and Nik. The rest of you are equally capable, and you'd all be just as good to choose, but—"

"No need to apologize, dude," Neil smiled. "You guys go rock this! We'll be chillin' out here."

Zoltan went up to the door. The instant he started opening it, the little light in the ceiling turned off (making everything pitch black.) There were no lights on the other side of the door either, so they'd have to feel their way along using the walls.

Frederick put his hands on Zoltan's shoulders. Then Peter went after him, gripping the back of Frederick's shirt.

Just as Nicola was about to put her hands on Peter's waist to join the procession, she felt someone slip past her.

"What??" she started to ask.

"Sorry, Nik," Valerie said, grabbing Peter and pushing him (and herself) through the door. "But trust me on this, they're gonna NEED me for whatever is down there."

As Nicola began yelling, "Get out of there!" at Valerie, a small light turned on in the new part of the hallway. She started forward to grab Valerie's arm and pull her back, but before she reached her, a gate dropped down from above, stopping her from proceeding.

Everyone was stunned. Valerie had forced her way into the 4-member group. What a selfish act...

"Val, you heard me say Nik was coming," Peter said sharply to her. He was about to continue scolding her, but a little voice inside his head pointed out that *what was done was done*, meaning an extensive yelling was just a waste of his breath.

"I'm so sorry, Pete," she said, eyes tearing up. "I don't know what got into me there."

"Nik," Peter said through the gate, completely ignoring Valerie. "What she did was wrong. Very wrong. But there's no way to undo it."

"She hasn't solved anything today!" Nicola complained. "She's only here because she likes you!"

"Are you romantically interested in my friend?" Frederick asked, turning to face his sister. "Not cool, Val. Not cool at all."

...

"Enough!" Claire then yelled, silencing everyone. "Look, the only thing we are doing now is wasting time. Go finish this. You can re-engage in your *debate* later."

* * *

Fighting back the frustration instigated by Valerie, Peter turned and started heading toward the next challenge. Valerie (now regretting what she'd done) ran to catch up and take his arm in support, but Peter swatted her hand away.

* * *

The room it led to was the most dangerous one they had been in so far today.

The square room, which was 5-by-5 meters in size, had ancient stone walls (which were covered in cobwebs and ugly moss.) And the stench being emitted here was atrocious.

They could see a locked gate on the far side: no doubt the goal of this test. And on the wall of the exit (high up near the ceiling) were the outlines of eight big numbers: *1, 2, 3, 4, 5, 6, 7, 8.* Each number was half a meter high and thirty centimeters wide, and appeared to contain lights that would likely turn on or off.

But it was the side walls in here that contained the most bizarre and confusing thing...

At about knee level, on both side walls, there were four 20-by-20-centimeter bricks, which were (of course) part of the walls themselves.

(All of those eight bricks were labeled with numbers.) The four on the left wall (starting closest to the entrance and going toward the exit) were labeled *1, 2, 3,* and *4.* There was roughly a meter gap between each one, meaning they were spaced out equally. And the right-side ones *(5, 6, 7,* and *8)* were in reverse, *5* being closest to the exit and *8* closest to the entrance.

And each one of the eight bricks had a thick chain attached to it. The end of each chain (all of which were about a meter and a half long) simply lay on the stone floor. The ends resting on the floor had handles attached to them, similar to the ones you would see hooked onto the cables of exercise machines at the gym.

* * *

Zoltan went over to inspect one. "Pretty heavy," he said while lifting it. "But if I use both hands, and lift with my legs instead of my back, I should be able to get it off the ground. Then I could pull on it to see what happens."

Zoltan heaved on the heavy chain attached to the 2-brick, lifting it off the ground. Then he leaned backward until the chain became taut. The brick seemed to pull out about five centimeters from the wall, but it wouldn't come out any further.

"Gotcha," Zoltan nodded, understanding things a little better now. As soon as he stopped leaning backward, the 2-brick returned to his original, flush position. "Not so complicated, is it?"

"But how do we, um... get this puzzle to start?" Frederick asked. "I'm assuming the eight large numbers above the exit will light up and tell us which bricks to pull?"

"I don't see rules written anywhere here," Valerie commented softly, fully aware now that she shouldn't have shoved past Nicola to be part of this foursome.

"Uh oh," Peter said, looking down at his beeping wristband. "Xavier's group just finished challenge four."

"As much as I despise my brother," Zoltan told his team. "I would be lying if I said he wasn't clever... I'm not surprised they are doing this well."

"Then it's time to show that *Xavier loser* that he pales in comparison to Pete," Frederick smiled. "Let's make him eat our dust!"

"Thanks," Peter grinned.

"Guys," Valerie said next. "I might be onto something about how to get the challenge to start. I think the sign on the door we just came through,

Only 4 continue, might be a hint. What if that has two meanings? One, that *only 4* team members move on. And two, telling us to pull on the *4*-brick to *continue."*

"Give it a go," Peter told her. "Nice thinking."

Valerie didn't look very strong or athletic, but she did manage to lift the heavy chain and pull it back far enough to get the 4-brick out of the wall a few centimeters.

"Starting sequence!" a computer voice loudly announced.

They looked at each other in confusion, not knowing how to react.

But when the 7-light on the far wall turned on, they were pretty sure what was happening.

Zoltan was the closest to that one, so he picked up the chain connected to the 7-brick and leaned back with all his might.

The 7-light then turned off, and the 8-light came on next.

Zoltan released the *7* while Pete ran to the 8-chain.

Bzzt!

"Failure!" the robotic voice announced right after the loud buzzer sounded.

"Um..." Frederick mumbled. "That was weird.

Pete didn't even have a chance to pick the chain up."

...

"I think we need to place ourselves in better positions," Frederick then suggested. "Let's all stand in the middle, in a line. I'll be at the back, near the entrance, by the 1 and 8 chains. Pete, you go in front of me, so you are in charge of the 2 and 7. Val watches the 3 and 6. And Zoltan, closest to the exit, has the 4 and 5."

"Nice," Peter smiled.

* * *

Once they were in the positions Frederick had just outlined, Zoltan pulled on the 4-chain to start the sequence for a second time.

"Beginning sequence!" the computer announced again.

Peter was assuming the 7 would once again turn on first, so he already had both hands on the handle.

He was right! The 7-light did turn on!

...

Just like last time, the 7 then turned off, and the 8-light came on next.

Freddy (the weakest one on their team) strained hard to get it off the ground. Knowing he couldn't fail, he heaved with all his might and managed to do it.

Peter, while watching Freddy struggle, actually forgot to let go of his chain.

...

The 8 turned off.

And then the 7-light turned on again!

Freddy, of course, let go of the *8*. And since Peter was already pulling on the *7*, he just kept doing so.

Bzzt!

...

"What!?" Frederick complained. "Pete was holding the 7 the whole time! What did we mess up?"

"Pete, I think I have a theory of what's going on," Valerie commented. "There's a possibility that none of the bricks can be released until the full sequence is complete."

"Ah," Peter said, nodding. "But that's not gonna be easy. These things are heavy..."

"Then let's switch up our positions a bit," Zoltan suggested. "Freddy, you come up to where I am, and I'll go back where you are. We know the 8 is going to be on for a while, so I'll be in charge of holding it."

"Let's hope that the *third time's a charm* thing works here," Peter then joked. "And give me another thirty seconds to recover before we start. I wanna make sure my arms are up for this."

…

Their third attempt was going very smoothly. Peter and Zoltan were pulling hard on the *7* and *8,* and everyone was eager to see what the fourth light would be.

The 4-light came on.

"That's one of mine!" Frederick said, pulling on it with all his might.

…

But the gate didn't open…

…

And no more lights came on…

"I can't hold mine any longer!" Peter (whose whole body was trembling) whined. Then he dropped the heavy chain.

No one voiced their disappointment, but they didn't need to: it was written all over their faces.

Not only were they still confused, but this test was also taking a toll on their bodies.

What they currently knew was as follows: One, pulling the 4-chain started the sequence, which was identical each time. Two, none of the blocks could be allowed to return to their original positions during the sequence. And three, the 4-digit sequence was *7 8 7 4.*

Hi READER!
HERE'S A HINT: PART OF THE SOLUTION IS HIDING IN THE NUMBERS *7 8 7 4...* ANY IDEA WHAT *"7 8 7 4"* COULD POSSIBLY MEAN?

"Okay, guys," Frederick said, pencil and paper ready. "Anyone have an idea what *7 8 7 4* might represent?"

"I might sound a little like Nicola here," Zoltan said next. "But how about relating the numbers to letters?"

Frederick quickly jotted down Zoltan's train of thought.

$A = 1$
$B = 2$

$C = 3$

$D = 4$

$E = 5$

$F = 6$

$G = 7$

$H = 8$

$7\ 8\ 7\ 4 = G\ H\ G\ D$

...

Seeing numbers correspond to letters somehow set off a positive cascade of synapsis in Valerie's mind. "Freddy, give me your pencil and paper, quickly!" she said, frantically writing something down.

...

"What are you working on?" Frederick asked her.

"Remember puzzle eleven from our book?" Valerie smiled.

"Sure," Frederick answered. "The one where pushing the buttons on a phone, to spell out a word, was the solution."

Valerie smiled even bigger.

"Hey, I think I get what you mean," Peter said after overhearing that. "All numbers on phones contain letters. And it's universal. You know, the

2-button always has *ABC,* and the 3-button has *DEF,* et cetera."

Valerie showed Peter what they were dealing with.

7: *P Q R S*
8: *T U V*
7: *P Q R S*
4: *G H I*

She then crossed out some of the letters (that definitely couldn't be used to spell a word.)

7: *P Q̶ R S*
8: *T̶ U V̶*
7: *P̶ Q̶ R S*
4: *G̶ H I̶*

Peter then crossed out a few more.

7: *P Q̶ R S̶*
8: *T̶ U V̶*
7: *P̶ Q̶ R̶ S*
4: *G̶ H I̶*

"That leaves us only two possible words," Valerie commented. *"RUSH.* Or *PUSH."*

"Rush or push, eh?" Frederick nodded, thinking deeply. *"Rush?* We've been rushing the whole time, so it can't be that... Then *push?* But *push* what?"

Valerie thought back to one of her favorite one-box comics ever: a hilarious one showing a clever kid who was about to enter a school for the gifted, but couldn't get in the door because he was pushing on it (even though the door was clearly labeled *PULL*.) Of course, this joke struck a chord with her, since she also excelled academically but messed up on simple, everyday things...

"Talk about tricky," Valerie said, shaking her head. "We aren't supposed to pull on the bricks, we have to PUSH on them. ... So why are there chains on all eight then, huh? When technically only the 4-brick, which has to be pulled to start the sequence, needs a chain? ... Simply put, they are red herrings, meant to throw us off. They were trying to make us *assume* the bricks should be pulled."

"Nice deduction skills," Zoltan said, commending Valerie's great work.

"But let's make sure I'm right before celebrating prematurely," she told everyone.

* * *

When they were all back in the same positions as before, Frederick pulled on the 4-chain to start the sequence again.

This time, when the 7-light turned on, Peter (who was sitting cross-legged right in front of the *7)* pushed it back hard with both hands. It moved back into the wall about five centimeters.

Zoltan did the exact same thing for the *8* after

seeing the 8-light.

When the 7-light turned on again, Peter just kept pushing.

"Get ready, Freddy," Valerie said to her brother. "Hey, that rhymed." She giggled at her unintentional humor.

(But this was definitely not the ideal timing for a pun…)

Freddy pushed the 4-brick the instant he saw the 4-light come on. (And then they all looked nervously at the locked gate.)

…

It began rising!

"Yahoo!" Peter yelled. "But don't stop pushing yet! Wait till it's completely open!"

When the gate had receded all the way into the ceiling, Peter doled out some instructions. "Everyone go through it as fast as you can!" he explained. "We have no idea how this thing works… For all we know, the gate may start coming back down the second we stop pushing. Okay, on three… One, two, three!"

Valerie (who was not in charge of pushing a brick) was already through before Peter had finished the countdown.

The other three got up and dashed for the exit.

The gate, thankfully, didn't start moving again—meaning that even Peter (who tripped over one of the chains and fell while running) made it out easily.

Good job, team!

CHAPTER 35

The poorly lit tunnel they entered turned out to be fairly long. And as it curved back and forth a few times, this dark path also appeared to be heading slightly upward.

***

"There's the end of the tunnel!" Frederick announced when he finally spotted the door they were heading toward. "It looks like there's a sign on it, but there isn't enough light to see it from here: I'll need to get closer."

When they all got to the door, they could easily make out the very simple message on the sign.

Only 2

"I suppose that means Freddy and I are stopping here, right?" Valerie said, taking Peter's hand.

"Yeah," Peter told her. "But odds are this is the last test. It won't be long before we come back for you."

Valerie took Peter's other hand as well.

...

"Umm... Val?" Frederick said to his sister. "Look, umm... maybe this is none of my business, but let me put it this way: What would *YOU* think if *I* tried to pick up one of *YOUR* new friends?"

(Wow, that was pretty direct!)

Valerie knew the point her brother was trying to get across, but she had already made up her mind about how much she liked Peter.

"Freddy," she replied. "I know you think what I'm doing is weird, or wrong, or whatever... But Pete's only seven and a half months younger than me. The age difference between me and him is less than between him and you."

"I'm not talking about your ages," Frederick said back.

"And you know I've never dated anyone in my entire life," Valerie went on. "Because I had never found the perfect guy. Now I have, so I'm not wasting my chance."

"Val," Peter said, looking her in the eyes (and realizing how happy he was to hear her confession...) "Of course, I, uh... like you, but let's put things on pause until—"

"Until when?" she asked him, concerned.

"I just mean until after Zoltan and I finish these puzzles," he answered.

Valerie leaned in and kissed him on the lips, (right in front of her brother!)

"Then hurry up and finish them," she pleaded, releasing his hands so he could continue onto the next puzzle.

* * *

As Peter and Zoltan began walking through the unlocked door, Peter seemed to exude some newfound confidence, both as a champion puzzler and a "sought-after man." A slightly older woman, who was amazingly intelligent and stunningly beautiful, really liked him. (And for some reason, he didn't feel intimidated at all by that fact... This could lead to a relationship unlike he had had before!)

(But back to the puzzles first, Peter! C'mon, focus!)

As soon as the spring-loaded door closed behind them, lights came on to unveil they were in a 4-meter-wide, round room, which had a high ceiling (going up at least five meters.)

"You see an exit?" Peter asked Zoltan (knowing fully well he would reply with a "No.")

In addition to the lack of exit, there was no hint or clue in here either.

The one (and only) thing they did understand

was where they were expected to stand: There were two circles marked on the ground, each a diameter of about 75 centimeters.

The circles were spaced about two meters apart. One had a large yellow *1* on it and the other was labeled *2.* There was also a thick chain, one end fixed to the *1-circle* and the other to the *2-circle.*

"I would usually suggest we inspect things more thoroughly before beginning," Zoltan said to Peter. "But there's not much in here to look at, is there?"

"Plus, we are in a race," Peter added. "One that we are currently leading, but who knows how long for…"

* * *

Peter stood on the *1* and Zoltan stood on the *2.* Then they heard a loud click.

The two circles began rising from the ground, higher and higher and higher. The grinding noise being made as these pillars extended was deafening, echoing endlessly around the high chamber.

* * *

When they finally stopped (at a height of over two meters), Peter noticed that his wristband was beeping again.

"Xavier has just caught up to us," he relayed to Zoltan.

"Okay," Zoltan nodded. "And Peter, best not to look down…"

"I'll try not to," Peter replied. "But then where exactly am I supposed to look?"

A few seconds later, a small circle opened up on the wall (at a height fairly close to where their waists currently were.) A long, steel pole started extending out of the hole, and was coming toward them at a constant pace, (indicating it was being powered by a machine and not a person.)

When the end finally got close to where Peter was standing, he could see a single word had been engraved on the end of the pole.

WAIT

"Peter, what does it say?" Zoltan asked, unable to see the small letters from his position on the *2-pillar.*

"This is the shortest clue we've ever had," Peter told him. "There's only one word: *Wait.*"

"Wait?? Wait... for what?" Zoltan asked Peter.

"Good question," Peter agreed. "If we can answer that, I bet we will be walking away victorious."

CHAPTER 36

(WAIT??) ...

...

HI READER!
ANY IDEA WHAT ZOLTAN AND PETER NEED
TO DO HERE?

"Peter," Zoltan called across from his pillar (which he was now sitting on to counteract his fear of heights.) "My intuition is telling me one thing, but it goes against today's competition in every sense."

Peter tried to decipher the meaning of that comment, but couldn't. "Sorry, that went in one ear and right out the other," he told Zoltan.

"Here's what I think *WAIT* is referring to," Zoltan started to explain. "In order to win, one must, well... *wait.* What I mean is that whoever solves the final challenge first, in reality, loses...

The winner is the one who can *WAIT* for the other team to solve it first.

"Um…" Peter pondered. "Are you saying the solution is to NOT solve it?"

(Yikes, now they were both confused!)

"Well, I can say this," Zoltan then told Peter. "One essential element of being a good puzzler is to never allow impatience to alter one's decision-making. I think that value is being directly applied to this test."

"So you just want to… uh, stand here?" Peter asked. "And do nothing?"

"Or sit, like I already am," Zoltan laughed.

* * *

The minutes were now going by excruciatingly slowly. After only four minutes of this "do nothing" approach, Peter was already starting to go crazy…

"But I'm also completely fine if you have a different theory you would like to test out," Zoltan said to Peter.

"Don't fret," he smiled. "I've been pondering various ones the entire time."

* * *

Another long and slow five minutes went by.

"Zoltan," Peter then said. "I'm not suggesting that we abort your plan to *wait,* but, well… just hear me out."

"I'm all ears," Zoltan replied.

"I'd say there is one thing we have yet to give any consideration to," Peter explained. "The chain... Why do you think there's a chain connecting the tops of these two pillars? If we were simply expected to just sit here and wait, then the chain would be completely unnecessary."

"Very good point," Zoltan nodded in agreement.

Peter so badly wanted to pace around, as he knew that would kick-start his brain a little better. (But he had to settle for a cross-legged seat on his pillar).

Peter just kept reciting, over and over, the single-word clue:

WAIT

WAIT

WAIT

...

HI AGAIN, READER!
WHAT COULD *"WAIT"* POSSIBLY MEAN?

Peter stood up again (as his seated position seemed to be even less productive than when he had been standing.) Then he (somewhat foolishly) jumped up and down a few times to get his blood pumping.

"Don't lose your balance!" Zoltan scolded him. "You know I can't use my powers in here to save you if you fall."

After a few jumps, Peter stopped…

Then he looked down at the circle he was standing in…

(Was Peter onto something??)

"Zoltan!" Peter yelled over, in a tone showing he had indeed noticed something promising. "Jump and down on yours, too!"

"No way," he said back. "I'm not stu—-"

"Just do it!" Peter *ordered* him.

Zoltan, reluctantly, did as instructed.

…

"Did you notice it?" Peter asked eagerly.

"If you are referring to the fact that the pillar briefly shifts down a few centimeters each time I land on it?" he said back." Then yes, I certainly did. But I don't see how that—-"

…

(WAIT)

…

"Whatever is holding these pillars high up here must be fixed to some type of, I don't know, *spring contraption* in the ground," Peter told Zoltan. "If we can apply enough force to the top of the pillar, like the impact from a jump, and do so constantly, then we might be able to push these back down to where they started."

"But other than jumping," Zoltan commented. "What else can we do? As you just pointed out, the downward displacement we cause during each jump only lasts for a second. It's nullified right away when we launch ourselves in the air for the next jump."

"Somehow, we need to apply more weight," Peter said, thinking. "We need weight."

...

...

"Oh, my..." Peter then grinned, shaking his head. "This puzzle contains a word trick! Don't you see it? They gave us a word that can be pronounced the same even when it's spelled differently... W-A-I-T and W-E-I-G-H-T are pronounced the same!"

"So the word *'WAIT'* on that pole is actually telling us to add *WEIGHT?*" Zoltan asked. "But where do we get more weight from?"

HI READER!
WHAT IS PETER ABOUT TO SUGGEST?

"Easy," Peter smiled. "One of us uses the chain to move over to the other guy's platform. If we are both on the same one, we'll essentially double the *weight* being applied."

"Um," Zoltan said, looking at the 2-meter drop to the floor below. "But who moves and who stays?"

"Hmm, don't know," Peter answered. "We'll just have to test both. But that should be simple, since there are only two."

...

Only two...

Only 2??

"The sign on the door!" Zoltan exclaimed. *"Only 2!* Maybe that means we both have to stand *ONLY* on the *2!"*

...

Peter's legs were pretty weak, but his arms were even weaker. Dangling on a chain and then going across arm over arm like a monkey was not going to be easy.

(But almost all people, when put in high-pressure situations, seem to magically muster the energy necessary to survive.)

* * *

Peter was happy that the girth of the chain links was the perfect size for a human hand to grip. And they had also been coated in something to make them less slippery.

As soon as Peter was hanging from the chain (very close to where he had just been standing on the 1-pillar), the pillar Zoltan was standing on slowly started to lower.

"I think it's working!" Zoltan cheered. "Maybe you don't even have to come over here. It seems like half of your weight—which is now being applied to my pillar because you're hanging from the chain—is doing the job!"

...

"But hold on," Zoltan said when his pillar had gone down about 50 or 60 centimeters. "The chain is almost stretched taunt now. Mine can't keep lowering unless yours starts lowering as well."

(Uh oh...)

...

Click

"Peter! Look!" Zoltan yelled excitedly. "BOTH pillars are now moving down! I guess getting mine to lower about half a meter triggered some type of switch."

Peter, glad that this problem had been solved without any additional thinking, held on tight (happy to see his feet getting closer and closer to the ground!)

But when he touched the ground (and let go of the chain), both pillars began rising again!

"Quick! Grab the chain again!" Zoltan told him. "And lift your legs off the ground, too!"

As soon as he did this, his weight caused both pillars to start lowering again.

"Maybe you do have to get up on mine after all," Zoltan suggested. "Keep your hands and feet on the chain, and *sloth* your way over here."

Zoltan's pillar was only about thirty centimeters off the ground when Peter reached it. He was hanging by the insides of his elbows and knees, doing everything possible to keep himself in the air.

They knew the upward motion would restart when Peter put his feet on the ground to get ready to jump on the *2...* But if he did this motion quickly, that might not matter.

...

"Welcome aboard," Zoltan said when Peter was on the 2-pillar with him.

This time, the empty 1-pillar started rising again, but the *2* continued to lower.

When the *2* got perfectly flush with the ground, they heard a strange popping or cracking noise. The place where the chain was connected to the 2-pillar had been preset to uncouple at this exact moment!

With the chain no longer attached to the *2,* the pillars were free to move independently.

Their pillar didn't stop when it was flush with the ground, it kept going and going, lower and lower.

"We had better hope this delivers us to the exit," Zoltan gulped. "Or else we'll be crammed in here like sardines for eternity."

* * *

And, thankfully, it did!

After their pillar stopped, more than two meters below the surface, a crawl-sized hole was right in front of them. This new tunnel would, no doubt, take them to the location of the amulet!

"You guys in there!?" Peter screamed down the long, narrow tunnel. (But he had forgotten their mouths were taped shut! They, of course, couldn't reply…)

Then he heard some dreadfully bad tap dancing.

"Sounds like Brad!" Peter smiled. "He's doing a tap dance version of, well, some dance only he knows."

...

"Okay, remember the plan?" Peter said to Zoltan, making sure neither entered the tunnel.

"Yup," Zoltan replied. "Man, I hope this works."

"Don't worry, it'll work," Peter said, reassuring Zoltan that this was what had to be done to finally rid the universe of Xavier.

CHAPTER 37

"Are you absolutely, positively sure this is the best way?" the overly concerned Zoltan asked Peter a few minutes later.

"Well, 99.99%," Peter replied, smiling. "Nothing in the world is a guarantee, right?"

Both Peter and Zoltan, still crammed together in what felt like a narrow well, stared non-stop at the band on Peter's wrist.

"As long as we don't start down that tunnel," Peter reminded Zoltan. "Then technically we haven't completed this challenge: meaning Xavier has no idea how far along we are."

"Ah," Zoltan nodded. "His wristband will only start flashing AFTER we enter the tunnel."

"Precisely," Peter replied. "But as you know, we aren't gonna do that until shortly after he completes this challenge."

"That's what worries me," Zoltan gulped.

From that point on, they waited in relative silence. They also took turns stretching their quads and hamstrings, as they didn't want someone to get a leg cramp at the most inopportune time.

* * *

"It's beeping!" Peter yelped, heartbeat skyrocketing.

Zoltan checked Peter's wrist to confirm that a sixth green circle was now on.

Xavier's tunnel was likely similar to Peter's: the only difference being that it entered the final chamber from the opposite side. (Unfortunately, they had no way of knowing if that assumption was fully accurate or not.)

"How long do we wait for?" Zoltan asked in a frenzy.

Peter was counting the seconds on his fingers. When he got through both hands twice, meaning 20 seconds had elapsed, he started crawling.

* * *

The tight tunnel turned sharply to the left about halfway through, and immediately after that bend, they could see the light from the chamber they were heading toward.

And they could hear Xavier's voice!

"Victorious!" Xavier bellowed, obviously already in the final chamber. "Looks like I have proven myself as the greatest puzzler of all!"

...

"Not so fast!" Peter yelled the second he and Zoltan reached the end of their tunnel. "We solved the last puzzle before you: We were just waiting back at the start of the tunnel."

"Balderdash!" Xavier mocked them, now standing where *Bridget,* Bradley, and Sophia were.

...

"Xavier," Zoltan said as calmly as he could, slowly inching closer to his evil brother. "Fine, the amulet is yours. We can accept that. But please don't use it to senselessly destroy worlds."

"Oh, listen to you, *goody two-shoes,*" Xavier groaned. "Have you suddenly discovered a new passion for helping others? Surely you haven't forgotten how much fun you used to get from torturing Earthlings?"

...

While they cautiously continued approaching Xavier, Peter scanned his surroundings carefully... (He was counting on this chamber containing a door that would allow them to exit the mountain without retracing their steps all the way back to the start.) ... And his assumption was correct!

"Stop right there!" Xavier's assistant, Orobas, yelled at Zoltan and Peter. "We won fair and square. The amulet is ours. One step closer and I'll clock the both of you." (He flexed his massive biceps to make his point.)

"Understood," Zoltan replied sadly, holding his arm out to stop Peter. "Then all I ask of you is this: let my young friends go free. Harming them would do nothing to help you build your new empire."

"Quite the contrary." Xavier barked back. "It will go to show everyone out there that my threats are always to be taken seriously... Orobas, film this."

Orobas removed a camera to record what was about to happen.

Xavier walked up to Bridget—well, the person he thought was Bridget—and hugged her.

"I'll untie you the second the amulet is in my hands," he told her, getting his key ready to open the box.

Xavier inserted the key, twisted it, opened the top, and looked inside. (There it was! The new amulet, which had yet to be used by any weather god, good or bad.)

"It's magnificent," Xavier said while carefully taking it out. "With this in my possession, the universe will bow to my every whim."

"Xavier," Zoltan pleaded. "Please allow me to untie these kids now."

"Be my guest," Xavier answered while doing

the same for *Bridget.*

Once Peter had his brother and sister's arms free, they both quickly ripped the tape from their mouths.

(But as planned, the girl impersonating Bridget left her tape on.)

"C'mon now," Xavier said to her. "Let me see that million-dollar smile of yours."

"Now!" Peter hollered, bolting to his right.

CHAPTER 38

Xavier's buddy darted after Peter.

Peter already had a good lead on him, and was sprinting toward the door he knew would allow them to quickly exit the mountain.

When Orobas realized he couldn't catch Peter, he turned around and focused on Bradley and Sophia instead.

Peter, meanwhile, pushed the heavy door open and was almost outside in the sunshine. As Orobas approached Peter's siblings, Sophia screamed in fear, and Bradley charged at him like an ox.

Upon impact, the much larger and stronger Orobas barely even budged from Bradley's attempted tackle.

Jakayla, the young woman pretending to be Bridget, removed the tape from her face and kicked Xavier in the shin as hard as she could.

"You evil, evil man!" she screamed at him, getting ready to sprint toward the door as well.

"An imposter!" Xavier yelled. "Where's my daughter!?" Then he paused to think...

"Orobas," Xavier said calmly to his assistant. "Allow them to go outside." Then Xavier smiled...

Zoltan, Bradley, Sophia, and Jakayla joined Peter outside the mountain. They were standing in a clearing between two peaks, with nowhere to run or hide.

Xavier and Orobas came out a few seconds later.

"Oh, I'm going to enjoy this," Xavier laughed. "What type of weather miracle shall I use to end your pathetic existence?"

Zoltan sent a wind blast toward the two evil weather gods.

Xavier's assistant quickly and effectively deflected it away. "Go ahead, my king," Orobas said, bowing to his leader.

Xavier, holding the beautiful new amulet in his hand, raised his arms high.

He began chanting...

The sky started to darken. The winds picked up.

(Uh oh, this was not good...)

Peter's team was focused: They had to wait for the ideal timing...

...

"Go!" Peter yelled. Peter and Bradley darted for Xavier.

Their attempt at a physical attack was so unsuspected that Xavier briefly lost concentration, and the clouds he had been conjuring up started to dissipate.

Orobas, beyond angry now, sent a powerful wind blast that knocked Peter and Bradley back a few meters.

Irritation showing, Xavier raised his arms again, preparing to command the weather to do something drastic.

He got an evil smile on his face, and continued chanting...

CHAPTER 39

But nothing happened!

"Xavier!" Orobas asked him, shocked. "What are you...? Are you alright?"

Xavier furrowed his brow and focused even harder. He was putting every bit of energy he had into this. He wanted to create a lightning blast big enough to incinerate them all!

But regardless of how hard he tried, nothing materialized!

"Look at the amulet!" Orobas yelled to his leader. "It's glowing green, and, uh... pulsating!"

Xavier had had his eyes closed, so he opened them to see for himself.

"Now!" Zoltan yelled.

Peter, Bradley, Sophia, and Jakayla ran full out at Xavier and Orobas, who were both *open* now because they were so distracted. Peter and

Bradley dove at the bigger and stronger Orobas while Sophia and Jakayla took down Xavier.

Zoltan, meanwhile, was creating a tight, powerful twister nearby.

Despite her small stature, Sophia's direct hit on Xavier's waist was perfectly on target. He had to release the amulet so he could use his hands to break his fall.

Jakayla dove and caught the amulet before it hit the ground. She quickly turned around and threw it toward the twister Zoltan was making.

The instant the amulet was in the tornado, Zoltan sent the tornado over the mountains, toward the ocean's edge, and continued pushing the twister until it was further away than the eye could see. Whenever the twister collapsed, it would drop the amulet into the ocean, where it would sink and be lost forever.

Peter and Bradley had managed to hold Orobas down for a few seconds, but not much longer. The big guy stood up again, yelled, and got ready to use his powers.

"Enough of this!" Xavier then screamed at the top of his lungs. "Orobas, leave them for me!" (Xavier wanted to be the one to kill the entire group.)

Xavier and Orobas watched Zoltan carefully while allowing the kids to run back to Zoltan's side.

"I hope you realize these two things," Xavier said loudly to his brother. "One, this will not stop me from achieving my goal of ruling the universe. Slow me down? Maybe. But prevent me? Absolutely not. And two, even without the amulet, I can easily end your lives. And that's exactly what I am about to do."

Xavier raised his arms to create a lightning bolt: one strong enough to fry them all.

...

"What's going on!?" Xavier screamed. "My powers aren't... I can't—"

"Xavier! Send your lightning blast!" Orobas begged of his leader. "We must prevail!"

Now that both were distracted again, Zoltan sent his own lightning bolts at them. Both hit their designated targets, intentionally only strong enough to stun them, though. (Zoltan was not a murderer.)

* * *

Zoltan then walked over and looked down at his older brother.

Zoltan hands were in his pockets. He removed what was inside one of those pockets, and showed it to Xavier.

"This can't be!" Xavier cried, completely baffled. "Then what did I just use—?"

"Not that I owe you an explanation," Zoltan laughed. "But I suppose telling you can't hurt."

Before saying any more, Zoltan made sure

Peter and his friends tied Xavier and Orobas' hands behind their backs. Then he had the two sit up.

"The thing you removed from the box, the box attached to the young woman who you now know is not your daughter," Zoltan went on, "was NOT the new amulet... it was the faulty one! I had a jeweler on Sevlar fit the faulty amulet into a custom stone casing that was identical in size and shape to the new amulet. Since the new one is so much bigger than the old one, that task was easy for him to accomplish."

"Faulty?" Xavier reacted. "What are you talking about?"

"Well," Zoltan went on. "The old amulet started acting up a little while ago. After some experimentation, we figured out what was happening: it was briefly absorbing people's powers, and then returning the powers to them the next time they used it."

"Absorbing powers?" Xavier said in shock, fear showing on his face for the first time ever.

"Yup," Zoltan said, looking his evil brother straight in the eyes. "If we had let you use it again, you would've got your powers back... which is why we took it when we did... Your powers are now locked in the old stone, which is lost at the bottom of the ocean."

Peter walked up beside Zoltan. "So not only do WE still have the new amulet," he added. "But you are powerless forever. Plus, you'll be in prison until the day you die."

"Power corrupts, dude," Bradley then said, mocking Xavier. "You caused your own demise."

"You fools..." Xavier then said. "Do you know how many followers I have? Do you think they'll just sit back and let this happen without putting up a fight? You'll regret what has happened here today..."

"Stand up," Zoltan said, ignoring his brother's scare tactics. "We are taking you down the mountain now, where you will inform the rest of your team what has happened. Unlike you, though, I have no intention of imprisoning anyone, other than you. The rest of your team will be allowed to leave peacefully."

Xavier stared into Zoltan's eyes. "Just remember this," he said coldly. "Whatever doesn't kill me can only make me stronger."

"Dude, zip it," Bradley remarked. "We are sick and tired of your stupid comments."

Peter high-fived Bradley, followed by the rest of the team. "Well said, my man," he laughed. Then he turned to face Xavier. "Your days of being a menace are over. O-V-E-R."

Zoltan unexpectedly passed the amulet to Peter.

"Don't you think you should hold onto this?" Peter asked him, a little confused. "You may need it to stave off any rogue attacks from Xavier's followers."

"Possibly," he replied. "But I think it's best to get it out of my hands for the time being. I might be tempted to use it to exact revenge on my brother before we even get him to prison."

Peter carefully placed it in his backpack. "Gotcha," he told Zoltan. "Now let's go home. I've had enough of this madness."

"You can say that again," Zoltan grinned.

CHAPTER 40

Close to three weeks had passed since their successful mission to rob Xavier of his powers and imprison him forever. And since that day, some other "weather god things" were improving as well.

After a long and thorough discussion with the Axon government, where Zoltan explained the truth about everything that had transpired, the leaders made a couple of big decisions.

The first was to allow Mr. Winchester (who was still wearing Zoltan's tracing band) and Klaron to return to Earth.

The second one, which would positively impact millions, was to restart communications between Sevlar and Axon after all these years, with hopes that talks might help bury the hatchet and build a healthy relationship going forward.

* * *

"Peter! The phone's for you!" his mom called upstairs from the family room.

"Okay!" he yelled back through his closed

bedroom door. "I'll get it on the upstairs cordless!"

* * *

A day or two after they had returned to Earth, thankful that their highly stressful "job" to keep Earth safe was FINALLY finished, Peter was kind of hoping to get the *fairy-tale ending* he thought he deserved. (Stories like this always end up with the hero getting back together with his or her first love interest, right?)

However, it would seem that fairy tale endings only happened in, well, *fairy tales...* (Peter had called Nicola twice to reconcile, but received a fairly cold reception during both of those short chats.) Therefore, he had concluded that a *"Peter-Nicola" reunion* just wasn't in the cards...

* * *

"Hey handsome," Valerie said once Peter had the receiver up to his ear. "How's it going?"

"Pretty good," he replied. "Although part of me is finding this history report A LOT duller than solving puzzles to save the world."

"We still on for later?" she then asked.

"You bet," he answered. "What time are you swinging by?"

"About eleven o'clock," she told him. "And make sure you bring lots to drink: we're gonna be hiking for hours."

"Prep is 100% done," he said.

"Just as I expected," Valerie laughed.

"Oh," Peter then said before she hung up. "Is

Freddy still... um, bitter about this?"

"About the fact that we are dating?" Valerie said to Peter. "He was at first, but now he seems more or less fine with it. It's probably no big deal because I don't go to the same school as you guys."

* * *

At half past eleven, Valerie and Peter pulled into the parking lot near the start of the beautiful mountain range they would be spending the afternoon trekking around.

"A kiss before we start?" she asked him (leaning in even before he had a chance to reply!)

Then, hand in hand, they started up the hiking trail.

* * *

"I suppose Nik hates my guts," Valerie said when they were taking their first pit stop. "She thinks I stole you away from her, right?"

For some weird reason, one Peter couldn't even comprehend himself, he had no qualms about being perfectly honest with Valerie. "She seemed pretty angry at first, but then she started talking to me again last week," he told Valerie. "We even occasionally hang out at lunch now. But she never mentions your name, if that's what you mean."

"If I were in her shoes," she told Peter, taking both of his hands. "I would have fought harder to keep you."

"Well, she did make one comment when I told her you and I were going to try being a couple,"

Peter mentioned.

"Which was…?" she asked curiously.

"She simply said, *'Go for it,'*" Peter answered. "But when I asked her what she meant by that, she wouldn't expand."

* * *

Their hike continued to the peak of this low-elevation mountain, where they were currently having a lovely picnic in the early afternoon sunshine.

"Peanut butter and jam sandwiches??" Valerie laughed when Peter pulled them out. "Not much of a connoisseur, are you?"

"Don't knock it till you've tried it," Peter smiled, taking a big bite. "What did you bring?"

"Couscous," she answered.

"Cous… what?" Peter asked. Then he looked at it closer. "Sure this isn't bird food?"

"Open wide," she told him, bringing a spoonful of couscous close to his mouth while imitating a feeding technique so many parents used on infants. "The train is arriving at the station!"

But instead of being met with a mouthful of healthy food, Valerie pressed her lips up against his!

…

"You don't know how happy I've been since meeting you," she told Peter. "I thought guys like you didn't exist."

***

"Anything new in the *weather god world?*" Valerie asked as they started their descent back to her car. "Those from Chonostil have all gone back to their planet already, right?"

"Yup," Peter replied. "And the Sevlarians are set to depart tomorrow: That's why we're gonna drop by in the morning, so we can say our farewells."

"Think you'll miss them?" Valerie asked (knowing perfectly well he would.)

"Definitely," he admitted. "But at least I won't have to spend my evenings and weekends figuring out how to protect humanity."

"True," she nodded. "But there's one thing that's been kind of eating away at me."

"What's that?" Peter asked.

"Weather gods occupied a large portion of the Stoneburg Royal for months on end," she said. "That would have cost a fortune."

"Mr. Winchester and Zoltan gave them the money to pay," Peter told her.

"But where did THEY get all that cash?" she asked.

"Hmm... never really thought about that," he nodded, agreeing that this was a bit odd. "Let's ask them tomorrow."

"And speaking of Mr. Winchester," Valerie said next. "Has he decided to keep living on Earth? Or is he going to head back to Sevlar?"

"Well, he has no relatives there," Peter replied. "And since we are his closest thing to family, he's gonna stay here, at least for now."

"So after Zoltan's group departs tomorrow," she commented. "Then Mr. Winchester will be the only *non-Earthling* you'll be in contact with?"

Peter then stopped and unzipped his backpack. "Thanks for reminding me," he said while removing the amulet. "I need to return this to Zoltan before he departs."

"Isn't it crazy to think that this softball-size rock is capable of so much?" she asked.

"Totally," Peter agreed.

"Since you'll never see the amulet again, let's have some fun first," Valerie suggested, pulling out her video camera. "I'll take a movie of you pretending to be a weather god: We can give it to Zoltan as a farewell gift."

"Cool idea," Peter reacted. "He'll love it!"

Trying to be as silly as possible, Peter pulled his windbreaker hood up over his head. He also put on sunglasses in an effort to look a little more *mysterious.*

Valerie, camera in hand, then loudly announced, "Dearest weather god friends! I present to you... the one... the only... P P P PETER!"

Peter started giggling.

Peter (whose acting skills were atrocious) then "dramatically" removed the amulet from his pocket and held it closer to the camera.

Copying what Mr. Winchester had done many years ago when making Peter a video to display Zoltan's powers, Valerie then made a *request.*

"How about an earthquake, Peter?" she asked loudly.

Peter shook his head.

"A tornado then, perhaps?" she asked next.

He shook his head again.

"Then at least cook me up a storm!" she pleaded, laughing like crazy.

Peter nodded.

Peter had long since remembered the incantation used to create a thunderstorm, since he had heard it countless times over the past few years.

He pretended to concentrate, raised both arms high, and repeated the incantation Zoltan always used.

...

A light breeze suddenly blew, causing Peter's hood to blow off his head, exposing his giggling face. (What amazing timing! It almost looked real!)

Valerie had trouble keeping the camera steady because she was cracking up.

Peter closed his eyes and continued.

...

The clear, blue sky then turned grey... and loud thunder boomed!

Wait...

WHAT!?

The thunderclaps were enough to make Peter open his eyes. When he saw the massive storm surrounding them, his heart almost stopped. He looked at Valerie, who was shaking in fear.

Peter squatted down, lightly placed the amulet on the ground, and took a few steps backward.

Within twenty seconds, the storm vanished.

Then Peter fainted!

CHAPTER 41

When he came to, Valerie was sitting cross-legged on the ground, with Peter's head resting on her lap.

"Are you okay?" she asked her dazed and confused boyfriend.

"Umm... I, uh, think so," he answered.

"We both know that YOU just conjured up that storm," Valerie said (stating the obvious.) "That means this amulet can be used by regular people too, not only weather gods."

"No," Peter replied. "Mr. Winchester told me, very specifically, that only those from Sevlar or Axon, with weather god DNA, are capable of altering the weather." Then he stopped talking, swallowed hard, and looked straight at Valerie. "Well, it would appear I have something more important than the hotel fees to ask Zoltan and Mr. Winchester about tomorrow morning..."

"We're not waiting until then!" Valerie said, pulling Peter up.

"But this doesn't make any sense," Peter commented, completely confused. "I'm human... I was born on Earth... There's no way I can command the weather, that's ridiculous."

Valerie then cracked a little smile. "My boyfriend..." she remarked. "Not only cute and smart, but also with secret superpowers?? You are definitely one-of-a-kind!"

Thank you for reading *Unbelievably Puzzled.* I hope you enjoyed following Peter and his friends on their wild, puzzle-filled adventure! And I would be extremely grateful if you left a review for it on Amazon or Goodreads. Thank you so much!

Sincerely,

P.J. Nichols

What's Next??

You might be wondering, "Is The Puzzled Series done? Or will the adventure continue?" Well... I'm hoping that you can help me decide!

Actually, my original plan was to "wrap up all loose ends in the plot," and end the series with Book 9. But since these stories are still so much fun to write, I threw in that *little surprise* at the end of Book 9, thus "leaving the door open" for a few more books, (but only if that's what the readers are hoping for!)

So I'd like to ask you all a quick favor: What do you think? Would you like to see a few more Puzzled books? (Or is it time for me to begin a brand new adventure series?)

Please let me know (pj@pjnichols.com) what you think!

And while I wait to hear from everyone, I'll get started on a new mystery series, which will be an adventure story with a "detective twist" to it!

Thank you so much!

PJ

Manufactured by Amazon.ca
Bolton, ON

30844072R00125